"How is . . . what?"

"Your brandy."

"Oh. Sharp. No, sweet . . . uh . . ."

"Let me taste." She tried to raise the glass but his thumb and finger circling her wrist stopped her. "Open your mouth, Kyla. Let me taste."

Her response was ungoverned by thought. She lifted her face to him, her lips separating and her eyelids growing heavy, then falling as she sank into the moment. Through the fan of her lashes she watched his tongue seek her mouth. He licked the sticky residue from her lips, taking the taste into his own mouth to savor."

"Delicious . . . very sweet." He rubbed her chin with his thumb as he kissed her again. He searched for brandy from every droplet in her mouth until she had only the flavor of herself to offer him. As her legs began to weaken, Luke caught her behind the knees and lifted her into his arms, then carried her to the sofa. "Don't be frightened, Kyla," he groaned as she moved to pull away from his next caress. "I'll stop whenever you ask me to."

"Then stop here and now," Kyla begged in an urgent whisper.

His eyes met hers. "I have to start before I can stop."

"No, Luke—"

"Yes, Kyla, yes." And he molded his mouth to hers again . . .

WHAT ARE *LOVESWEPT* ROMANCES?

They are stories of true romance and touching emotion. We believe those two very important ingredients are constants in our highly sensual and very believable stories in the *LOVESWEPT* line. Our goal is to give you, the reader, stories of consistently high quality that may sometimes make you laugh, sometimes make you cry, but are always fresh and creative and contain many delightful surprises within their pages.

Most romance fans read an enormous number of books. Those they truly love, they keep. Others may be traded with friends and soon forgotten. We hope that each *LOVESWEPT* romance will be a treasure—a "keeper." We will always try to publish

LOVE STORIES YOU'LL NEVER FORGET
BY AUTHORS YOU'LL ALWAYS REMEMBER

The Editors

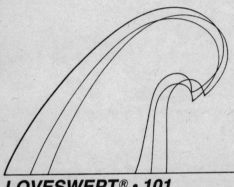

LOVESWEPT® • 101

Marianne Shock
Worthy Opponents

 BANTAM BOOKS
TORONTO • NEW YORK • LONDON • SYDNEY • AUCKLAND

WORTHY OPPONENTS

A Bantam Book / July 1985

ISBN 0-553-21711-9

Published simultaneously in the United States and Canada

---

*Bantam Books are published by Bantam Books, Inc. Its
trademark, consisting of the words "Bantam Books" and
the portrayal of a rooster, is Registered in U.S. Patent and
Trademark Office and in other countries. Marca Registrada.
Bantam Books, Inc., 666 Fifth Avenue, New York, New
York 10103.*

PRINTED IN THE UNITED STATES OF AMERICA

O   0 9 8 7 6 5 4 3 2 1

One

"I've been waiting for you." The owner of the soft baritone voice had crept up behind her.

Kyla froze. Standing on the sagging front porch of the locked-up store, her face pressed to the window, she didn't move a muscle. She didn't even breathe, so that the patches of fog she'd exhaled on the glass dried and disappeared. Forbidding mountain wilderness lay on either side of her. And behind . . . ? For the first time in her adult life, Kyla recalled her mother's fearful litany: *"Never talk to strangers, never open the door to a man, never . . . never . . . never . . ."* Twenty-three of her thirty years dissolved and Kyla was once again the timid little seven-year-old who'd cried at summer camp. This was going to be some vacation! she thought.

"You can stare in that window all day"—the voice, the *man*, had moved closer—"and you still won't find anyone. Turn around, love, I'm behind you."

Love? With diminished confidence and a shaky smile, Kyla glanced over her shoulder. Crystals of sweat streamed down his broad, stripped torso to dampen the waistband of low-riding jeans. Her brown eyes followed the smooth perfection of sculptured shoulders, up past the taut cords of his throat, to meet at last with arresting green eyes. A shock of lion's-mane hair was casually raked to fall where it might around a savagely stunning face. And to think *he* had been waiting for *her*, she marveled. Kyla's disobedient breath fled again.

His eyes moved over her, unsubtly touring the quiet curves beneath her khaki slacks and clinging knit top. Each willful curl of the dark hair tumbling to her waist knew the touch of those velvety jade eyes before he brought them to her face. "You're long overdue," he murmured.

Ignoring the steps, he vaulted to the wood-planked porch. Lord! He'd looked tall as Samson standing three steps below her. Now he towered over Kyla's five-foot-even frame. He was so leanly built that each relaxed muscle suggested a sleeping power. Kyla felt out of her element. Possibly out of her mind. Well, hadn't she hoped the mountains would be so foreign, so full of adventure, that she wouldn't have time to dwell on whether she'd get the promotion at work? And wasn't she finding exactly that!

At the same instant his booted foot scraped over the boards to bring him a step closer, her own foot carried her back. The stiff set of her spine stopped him in his tracks.

"Whoa, there. No need to bolt." His gaze softened, dropping to the white-knuckled fists pressed to her thighs. "Nothing to be afraid of. You're safe enough with me."

Kyla might have laughed if a lodged breath hadn't closed her throat. Safe? Frightened? Only to herself would she admit it wasn't fear that had her heart tripping over its own beat, nor fear that dropped her weight to the balls of her feet as if she were poised to dive from a cliff . . . or bolt. No, not fear. Fascination. For one rash instant Kyla had wanted to reach out and experience the warmth of his skin, the dampness of his chest, the hardness of his body. She wasn't at all safe!

Damn! Kyla gave herself a mental shaking. Primitive men didn't appeal to her. They never had. French cuffs and striped ties, yes. Not sinew and sweat.

She tipped her face up, setting her chin at a stubborn angle. The slight movement stirred her hair so that the sunlight's fire licked at the russet mane. "I'm Kyla Trent. I'm supposed to—"

" 'Bout time you found your voice," he interrupted in a lazy drawl. "And I know who you are." He leaned one shoulder against a rough-hewn post and crossed his arms and ankles.

"If you know who I am, you must know why I'm here." There. That sounded confident, she decided.

"In the mountains?"

"Uh . . . no. At the store."

"Mm-hmm," he murmured. "You rented Barry Michaels's cabin for the week and you've come for the key. I saw you hiking the lake path." The smile dancing in his eyes spread to his mouth, planting a boyish dimple in one rugged cheek. "Which means your car is either too old and decrepit or too racy and delicate to make the run on that potholed lane we call a road. And, like I said, I've been waiting a long time for you."

His husky last words dumped her stomach in her feet before Kyla remembered she was two hours behind schedule and his comment was addressed to that—and only that.

"Late start," she replied. He had the most disconcerting way of studying her mouth, watching her lips curve around words, making Kyla forget what she was going to say next.

"I called out to you a few minutes ago. Heard your boots knocking around on the floor planks. You didn't hear me?"

"No. All I've heard is a woodpecker tapping away at a tree."

A slash of blond eyebrows climbed an inch in astonishment. "Woodpecker? That was me chopping firewood!" His laughter was deep and rolling, and too pleasant to be taken for ridicule. "So it's a city girl I've got. Woodpecker!"

"*You've* got? Look, Mr. . . . ?"

He was laughing again, quietly, the sound gently tumbling around in that formidable chest. "Tenderfoot, you're about to spend a week stripped down to basics. I suspect you haven't a clue how to live the rustic life. You'll need the guidance of a knowledgeable native. In case you haven't noticed, it's pretty deserted around here." She'd noticed. "I'm all you've got." She'd noticed that too. "And that means *I've* got a city girl."

"You're assuming a lot just because I didn't know the difference between an ax and a bird." Oh, why bother? she thought. In truth she *was* a city girl, without the slightest idea how to survive the mountains. Kyla glanced at the plain wooden structure they stood in front of, then over the locked door at the hand-lettered sign: "POP'S ALL AND EVERYTHING."

It seemed an absurd question to ask a man of thirty-five or thirty-six years, but she had little choice. "Are you Pop?"

"No, he isn't." A weaker voice, gravelly and a bit breathless, announced the approach of a third person. "I am. And you must be Kyla Trent." Kyla pivoted on her boot heel as the store's owner labored up the steps to the porch. He was a small man, not much taller than Kyla. He had a thick, snowy beard and not a lick of hair on his head. And in the middle of all that white fluff, his pink lips were smiling. "That young man there is Luke Hudson."

Luke Hudson. The name fit the man, Kyla thought; both were strong and sturdy.

"She just got here, Jake," Luke told the man. Then the jade eyes gazed back down at Kyla. "He was next door with his wife. She's in bed with the flu.

Asked me to keep a lookout for you. He'll give you the spare key Barry leaves for renters."

Kyla nodded, her eyes fastened to Luke's. Pop was unlocking the front door and the moment arrived when she had to turn and go through it . . . or look like a damn fool if she didn't.

She tore her gaze away and turned toward Pop. Even with her back to Luke she couldn't seem to take that first step away. Control of her body, her breathing, her heartbeat, seemed to have slipped into his hands. What had gotten into her? Kyla wondered. Luke would wear a three-piece suit with the same ease another man might wear a straightjacket.

Kyla's internal chaos began to settle down when the drum of his step announced his departure. Then his voice stormed through her again, sending strange quivers to her stomach. "See you soon, Kyla."

Heaven help me, but I hope so, she whispered silently.

Kyla followed Pop into the store's dim interior. "He's a good boy, that Luke is," Pop said, shuffling to the sales counter on slippered feet. Kyla refrained from pointing out that that hard-packed, blood-and-muscle man could hardly be called a "boy."

"This here is your key." He scraped it across the counter. "Leave it in the dropbox out front when you go."

"I need a few things."

"Help yourself." Pop waved his arm at the well-stocked shelves. "Get everything you may need right now. Don't know when I'll open up again. Could be next Monday. My Beth needs me. 'Course, if it's an emergency, come and get me, I live next door."

Next Monday. Kyla's anxiety returned. This mountain vacation had successfully removed her from the office gossips and unending speculation, but there didn't seem to be a place on earth where Kyla could escape her self-doubt. Next Monday would find her locked in the crush of rush-hour traffic heading for her downtown Los Angeles office. As the new vice-president of CompuMart?

She wandered through the aisles, pushing a small cart. Pop's was half a dozen shops rolled into one: food and beverages, bait and tackle, mini-drugstore, camping supplies. Kyla stared at the ingredients on a can of chow mein; her mind's eye read the list of Chuck Myers's accomplishments. His regional sales figures were impressive. But better than hers? Probably not, she admitted. But he was fast. He could pick a client out of the Yellow Pages over morning coffee and sell him a computer line at lunch.

She put the chow mein back on the shelf and reached for a box of spaghetti.

Then there was Brad Upton. He had a broader, more diversified client list than hers. But her reorders were better, and reorders kept a computer-distribution company alive. Brad preferred the excitement of a new deal, the challenge of fast-talking customers into spending twice as much as they had intended. But Brad neglected them after the initial sale, put off upgrading their systems, she reminded herself. She dropped the spaghetti into her cart.

On a balance sheet, she thought, the three of them were pretty equal. But it was Kyla who had gone to the small computer manufacturers, convincing two of them to abandon direct-dealing with storefront retailers and let her distribute their lines through her larger national accounts. She was the only one who had thought to work both ends of the distribution chain. So what did Andrew Carson want in his next vice-president? Fast, flashy, or inventive?

Kyla heard the rip of metal and the whoosh of escaping air. "Here you go." Pop held out a sweating can of icy cola. "On the house. Take it back and keep Luke company while I total this up. Not too many young people up here these days." Then he added, as if it were a brand-new thought, "Not too many people up here at all, come to think of it."

To Kyla's surprise, the short counter was buried under her selections; she couldn't think what half of them were. Pop's trembling hand and myopic squint warned her it would be some time before the purchases would be rung up. She left the store, vowing to stop driving herself crazy about the promotion and enjoy her precious time off.

The lazy afternoon soaked up the California sunlight. Kyla glimpsed Luke's powerful arms heaving the ax, heard the resounding clunk as sharp steel invaded wood. Each report bounced against the surrounding mountain walls. Each repeating rat-a-tat echo faded as the next arc was completed, and the ricochet tapping continued. She cocked her head, listening: It did sound just like a woodpecker to her.

The tap of her boots on the floorboards turned his head. The brilliance of his strong, slashing grin slowed her footsteps. When she'd considered the dangerous attractions of the mountains, Kyla mused, a man like Luke Hudson had never occurred to her. She held the can of soda in one hand and tucked the other in her hip pocket to hide a sudden tremble.

"I've been ordered out," she explained. "Pop suggested I keep you company."

"Put 'er down over there," Luke said. The nod of his head indicated a set of steps leading to the store's screened back door. Resuming his attack on a section of log, he repeatedly laid the blade into it. With a sound of surrender, the wood split along its natural grain.

"How come an L.A. girl decided to hang out in the Sierras?" he asked, positioning another log on the chopping block.

"How do you know I'm from Los Angeles?"

"Except to a select few, this dying little community is virtually unknown. It didn't even merit a pinprick on the map."

"Why?"

"Why didn't it make the map?"

"No. Why is it dying?" Her gaze inspected the wild landscape, the blue-jewel lake, and the towering pines, their abundant boughs spread over cozy cottages. Her eyes glanced up the tall rock walls surrounding the little community, finding them as forbidding as they were protective.

"Original owners, most of them, are all about Pop's age. It's too far from help and hospitals. Only a handful of the second generation comes because the five-hour, straight-up drive sucks a tank of premium gas dry. For half the money, they can go to the ocean."

That's where she should have gone, Kyla chided herself. To the civilized ocean. "So you were saying," she prodded. "About my being from L.A.?"

"Mm-hmm. You've rented Barry's cabin, and since he doesn't advertise the place, you have to be a friend of his. And *he* lives in L.A."

Kyla shook her head. "Never met him. We have a mutual friend."

She finished off the warming soda and set the can down on the step. With both hands she lifted the hair clinging damply to her neck, giving the thick length a good shake. Red highlights in the undisciplined mass were repeated in her wide-set eyes, lending their brown depths a glow of banked fires.

"You didn't answer me," he persisted. "Why did Kyla Trent come to the mountains?" Every muscle in his back and upper arms flexed in answer to another bite of the blade.

Kyla suddenly thought of a commercial slogan: Mountain grown—rich and full-bodied. *It's the altitude*, she decided. "That's a good question," she said a moment later.

"So give me a good answer."

Kyla shrugged. "You've already guessed this isn't my natural environment. Maybe that's what made the offer of the cabin so appealing." He studied her with those soft, bright eyes and a pleasant warmth enveloped her. "I figured the mountains would be exhausting, physically *and* mentally, so . . ." It was proving difficult to put into words. She frowned, her inner tension coiling again. She gave full attention to a scuff in her boot leather. "I just felt like a change of scenery," she finished lamely.

"And how do you like the scenery so far?"

Her eyes left her boot toe and skipped over the stretch of pine-needle carpet to his feet, which were planted apart for leverage. Her dark gaze lingered along the lean-muscled legs to the snug fit of his beltless waistband, then swiftly scanned the springy honey-blond hair covering his upper chest. Her visual journey ended at the angular features of a terribly attractive face.

"I like," she said in a husky tone. "I like it a lot, so far."

He seemed embarrassed by her blatant appraisal, which surprised her. Certainly he'd encountered approval from women before. The man could stop traffic, not to mention female hearts.

He buried the ax blade in the block, resting his weight on its bleached handle. "That was nice. I've never been mentally stripped quite so sweetly before. But I meant the tall trees, the picturesque lake, the clean air."

Kyla lifted one auburn brow at him. "So did I, Luke." Her voice carried the smile that softly parted her lips. "So did I."

"Mm-hmm," he murmured. "I'll just bet. So you like the scenery, but you prefer the city."

"I *understand* the city."

The back door banged shut behind Pop and he set a large grocery sack down near Kyla. Two more trips produced two more overstuffed bags. "When you're done with that, Luke, can you help our visitor get these home?"

"Sure, Jake."

Kyla pushed herself up from the step she was sitting on. "That's all right. I can manage two of them now and come back later for the last one."

"Put 'er down, Kyla," Luke commanded gently. "It's quite a hike to the cabin on a narrow path littered with fallen limbs. You can't carry those bags *and* watch where you're going." He cast a disapproving eye at the stylish heels of her boots. "I'll be just a few more minutes, then I'll run you home in my jeep."

Kyla slid a glance to the path, remembering the walk up there and how she had feared each snap of a twig could have easily been her ankle.

Pop squinted his eyes, scanning the register tape. Kyla suddenly realized she'd left her purse locked in her car, and that the car was parked at the side of the cabin. "That'll be thirty-nine-fifty," Pop informed her. Luke saw her futilely pat empty hip pockets, and he came forward, extracting two crumpled twenties from his own pocket.

"Go on, Kyla, put 'er down. You and I can settle up later when I get you home."

She dropped back down to the step and let Luke work in silence. Something about the balmy afternoon turned her whole being lethargic. She decided to drift with the feeling, languidly caressing Luke's magnificent body with her eyes.

And his hair! So fine and soft, the sort that fell back in place when ruffled by a crisp wind or frenzied hands. Kyla would have killed for such silky locks as a teenager. Her thick, untamed hair was all the vogue now; back then it had been considered frizzy. Not even her constricting chignons or her coronet of braids for the office could be called smooth or sleek; there was always a soft, wild cloud framing her face.

That and her mouth were, she felt, professional weaknesses. Her lips were a little too full and curved to pull into a determined line. Worrying the plump lower one with her teeth, she glanced again at Luke's mouth, tightly set as he worked. The creases scoring his cheeks and the web of fine lines at his eyes said he was a man to smile and laugh often, and an easy animal grace declared him master of his world. Kyla felt a surprising regret that it had to be these godforsaken mountains.

"What are you doing here, Luke?" she asked.

He gave her the full wattage of his smile. "Right now, splitting enough wood to get Pop through the winter."

"How else do you fill the time?" Kyla glanced around, seeing a lot of dense forest and empty clearings.

"Fish. Swim. Go to bed early. Sleep in late."

It would drive Kyla nuts. All that time to fill. She thrived on a day of back-to-back appointments, relieved by a business lunch and capped by dinner with colleagues. *Computerworld* and decaffeinated coffee went to bed with her. A pained expression wrinkled her forehead at the very thought of living a life away from the pressure-cooker tension.

Luke saw the frown. "What's wrong, Kyla?"

A growling rumble of hunger provided her answer. "I skipped lunch and drove straight through. If you're going to be much longer, I'll go ahead and brave the lake path."

"Last one," he promised, positioning his final victim on the block. "My Land Rover is parked on the side. Load it up and I'll join you."

He was as good as his word, timing his arrival to coincide with Kyla's drop into the passenger side. A faded denim shirt lay on the driver's seat and he shrugged into the second skin, fastening only two buttons and leaving the tails untucked.

"Hold on," he advised her, flashing that devastating grin. No sooner had he pulled out of the lane to Pop's than Kyla was bounced into his lap as the four-wheel-drive vehicle bumped in and out of a cavity in the road. The collision with his hard chest was an impact like no other Kyla had experienced. Tiny explosions sent prickles of pleasure racing under her skin. She spent the balance of the ride bracing herself with one arm extended to the dashboard.

In the smoother gravel drive at her cabin, Luke braked to a sliding halt, throwing up a cloud of dust that engulfed the jeep. It settled back down, coating the black satin finish of her parked Jaguar with an ashy blanket.

Luke peered through the dispersing cloud and nodded as his eye fell on the sleek car. "Too delicate."

"I was forewarned," Kyla explained, referring to the road. "Although I'll admit it looks harmless from here and I nearly tried it."

"Be a good tenderfoot and don't try anything you're not sure about in these mountains. And never do anything you're told *not* to do. A lame car is the least of possible consequences."

"Yes, sir!" Kyla responded flippantly.

"I mean it, Kyla."

"So do I. I'm a coward to the core."

Luke gathered up the heavier two grocery bags while Kyla cradled the lightest one and moved ahead of him to unlock the side door of her temporary home. She bumped the door open with her hip and stepped into a small hallway, breathing in thick, stagnant air. Luke strode past her, obviously familiar with the cabin's layout.

"I was here yesterday," Luke said. "Filled the generator with gas and cranked her up so you've got electricity. And I turned on the hot-water tank for your shower." He moved to unlock and fling open a window over the sink, then repeated the process throughout the four-room structure as Kyla toured the cabin.

It was just as promised. Clean and compact, with lots of wood everywhere and windows facing the magnificent outdoor scenery. "Not so rustic," she called out to Luke. "Unpretentious maybe, but hardly primitive." She had a fantastic view of the lake from a pine-paneled living room and an intimate tree-enclosed patio just outside a door in the only bedroom. If there was peace of mind somewhere in the world, Kyla thought, this must be where it was hiding.

"Give me your car keys and I'll bring in your suitcase," Luke offered from the bedroom doorway.

Kyla dug the keys from her pocket and tossed them to his waiting hands. "Thanks, I appreciate that."

Minutes later he was back, hefting the executive-gray case onto the printed spread of a double bed. Kyla was inspecting the tiny blue-tiled bathroom. "Nice," she observed. "Very nice." She glanced over her shoulder to find Luke unsnapping the latches and opening her suitcase. "I . . . uh . . . think I'm . . ." She froze as he spied a scrap of satin and lace peeking out from under a navy sweatshirt. ". . . uh, going to . . . like it. . . ." He plucked the shimmery half-slip out of the case and— "Put it back," she whispered. The tour his eyes took made Kyla feel as if she were actually wearing the slip—and only the slip.

"Nice," he murmured. "Very nice."

"I said, put it back." She moved to his side, lifted the frothy lingerie from his hands, and slammed the suitcase shut. "I'll manage on my own now."

She crossed the room to the patio door, crushing the intimate garment to her chest, an uncommon fire burning her cheeks. A sticky knob resisted her for endless moments before she was able to fling open the door and suck in the cool mountain air. Luke left the bedroom and Kyla heard him next in the kitchen, unpacking her groceries.

"You are very persistent," she complained when she caught up with him. Taking a box of bran cereal from his hand, she turned him around by his shoulders and pointed him toward the door. "Thanks, Luke. Good-bye, Luke."

"But these are my goods," he insisted, solidly planting his feet and looking impossibly pleased with himself.

Kyla opened her mouth to argue, then remembered the forty dollars she owed him. "Sorry, I forgot," she admitted. "Let me get my purse from the car."

"I've done that already." Luke took the box from her hands and returned it to the table. Leaning past her, he introduced her to the hard heat of his body from shoulders to hips. It was an embrace without the use of hands or arms, but an embrace all the same. Time passed. Silence reigned. A sizzle of excitement ripped down her spine. Along with the earthy scent of his sweat, Kyla detected an intriguing trace of Luke's after-shave and the faint odor of tobacco smoke. He moved away, slowly, and not very far.

"It's buried under all that food," Luke said eventually. "Don't bother looking for it now. You can settle up with me later tonight. When I come for dinner."

"Dinner," she repeated thoughtfully. "I don't recall inviting you to dinner." Kyla felt control of more than just her evening being wrested from her. The feeling was so strong that her eyes dropped to his hands, convinced she'd find the reins of her life in them. A sprinkle of sun-bleached hairs covered the backs of his lean, tanned hands. His thumbs were hooked in his pockets, straining the worn jeans over a definite bulge. *Oh, Lord,* she thought, and closed her eyes.

"I'm inviting myself," he purred.

Steeling herself, she returned his provocative gaze. He cocked one brow, as if asking whether she liked what she saw, and added, "There's more than enough." Was he kidding? she thought wildly. His glance shifted to scan the pile of cans and packages and his mouth split with a cocky grin. "Why should both of us eat alone? You've nothing to worry about, tenderfoot." His rasping voice dropped an octave, his head several inches. His lips brushed her ear. "I'm a manageable beast. Not nearly as dangerous as the mountain's grizzlies and coyotes."

He's lonely, Kyla decided. Then—more reason to

say no! He's broke and looking for a free meal, she mused. A man who chopped firewood for a living wasn't eating steak. And it just so happened she had chosen a thick fillet from Pop's meat counter that could feed two if she served a generous salad.

And he *had* been nice to her.

And she could probably think up twenty more reasons if that's what it would take to talk herself into spending the evening with him.

"Feeding you is the least I can do," Kyla said slowly.

"Is that all I deserve? The least?"

"No. You'll get your forty dollars back too."

He dragged his thumb across her forehead, smoothing out a small crease of worry. "We'll have a good time, Kyla. It'll be fun."

By whose definition? she wondered. His long legs carried him out the side door but the tantalizing scent of male sweat lingered long after the sound of his jeep faded away. Had she lost her mind?

Kyla put the groceries away while the sun set in a glorious red-and-purple display. Leaving the steak in a pan to soak up her special sauce, she showered, then unpacked her clothes as a layer of moisturizer pampered her face and her loose, flowing hair was allowed to dry. Kyla always did two tasks at once and three if possible. She would have to stop that for the next week, she decided, pacing the living room, waiting for Luke to return at least twenty minutes before he was expected.

The salad was crisping in the refrigerator, the steak marinating. The table near the living-room hearth was set, draped with a white damask cloth Kyla had found in the linen closet. Matching napkins were pleated into spreading upright fans.

She would truly go crazy if the whole week passed as slowly as this half-hour. And to think she had filled her briefcase with the latest research on IBM compatible components and then purposely returned it to her spare bedroom/office, determined not to spend her vacation working.

She raked her fingernails over her scalp, fighting a physical itch to *do* something. Maybe she'd change her nail polish. She spread her fingers, considering the neutral, flesh-toned enamel. Not red. Red would clash with her flaming orange blouse. Pink? Ugh! Pink would be worse.

She ran damp palms over her hips, smoothing the white wool skirt. The mountain setting suggested the more practical attire of slacks. But she had been folding the slip Luke had touched and felt compelled to put it on, to have it hug her hips and slide along her thighs when she moved. She refused to dissect the reason behind such adolescent behavior.

The rumble of Luke's jeep returning invaded the stillness and Kyla rushed to fling open the door. Gold cabin light spilled out into the pitch-black night. The dense layer of pine branches prevented even the weakest shower of moonlight to diffuse through the trees. The jeep's headlights snapped off and the silhouette of Luke disappeared.

Then he entered the patch of light from the open door and Kyla struggled with a surprised breath. The cuffs of charcoal slacks brushed the tongues of expensive loafers. The collar of a pale pinstripe shirt, open at the throat, was folded over a pearl-gray sweater. *If he's hiding French cuffs under his sweater sleeves, I'm sunk*, she thought.

As he reached the threshold, Kyla issued a soft whistle, falling easily into the kind of equal footing that she shared with the men in her business life. "You clean up nice."

He bowed graciously and presented her with a bottle of California wine.

"Come in, Luke," Kyla said. "I'll put this on ice. Go on to the living room, I'll be right in."

Once Kyla had joined him, he asked, "How does it feel now that you're settled in?"

"It's a very . . . uh, casual way of life."

"Casual." He tested the word out loud and nodded. "I guess that would describe it. You're not finding it dull, are you?"

"Dull might also describe it." Kyla shrugged and smiled. "Culture shock. I'll adjust. Can I get you a drink? I found a well-stocked bar."

"Let me. What can I fix you?"

"Sweet vermouth on the rocks, thanks. I also found a radio that doesn't work. And there isn't a single newspaper or magazine in the place to read."

"You were supposed to be slaving over my dinner, not catching up on world affairs." He came toward her, his own Scotch in hand. She had laid out an assortment of foods to nibble on the low coffee table, and his interested gaze ran over the choices. Smiling, he picked up an empty cut-glass bowl and studied the salty remains in the bottom. "What's this?"

"Nuts. Deluxe mix."

"Thanks. I'd love some."

"Boredom, I guess." *Nerves*, she admitted to herself. When she was nervous she ate everything in sight. Taking the bowl from his light grasp, she returned it to the table.

He reached out with his free hand, manacled her wrist, and pulled her around to face him. "Hey, you're really uptight. And cold. Your hands are freezing. Does it frighten you, Kyla? Being alone with me?"

"My hands are cold because the cabin is cold. When the sun went down, so did the temperature, and I haven't been able to find the thermostat."

"That's because there isn't a furnace. I'll get a fire going, tenderfoot."

"Is that my only source of heat?"

"Mm-hmm." He slid the mesh screen open. "Be sure to open the flue if you try this yourself. Lay the kindling on the grate, place the wood on the kindling, light a match—"

"I know how it's done, Luke. Fireplaces are not

exclusive to the mountains. I'm just thinking how cold the rest of the cabin will be."

"You'll get plenty of heat from the fireplace."

Kyla took the empty nut bowl to the kitchen. She turned the steak in the marinade and tossed the salad while Luke saw to the fire. When she returned to the living room a billowing black cloud was filling the room.

"If I get as much heat as you got smoke, I'm all set."

"The chimney is blocked," Luke announced tersely. "Open the doors and windows." A rain of particles scattered into the grate, followed by the landing thump of whatever was lodged in the chimney. The flue began to draw properly.

"Is this the fun part?" Kyla asked in a voice rich with laughter. "Are we having a good time?"

"Just do as you're told, Kyla." He was *not*, she noticed, laughing with her.

For the next five minutes they coughed and fanned the acrid air until the smoke had cleared and they were able to close the doors and windows. Just as Kyla was returning to Luke and the much-needed warmth of the fire, the lights flickered once, twice, then the whole cottage went suddenly, ominously dark.

"Luke," she called tremulously. "What's happened? Why did the lights go out?"

She saw him in the scarlet reflection of the flames as he looked over at her. "Generator must have quit. I'll have a look at it."

Carefully moving around the furniture, he headed for the kitchen with Kyla right on his heels. He struck a match and held it over an open drawer while looking for a flashlight or candle to take with him.

Laughter bubbled out of Kyla. He was in no mood for it, but she couldn't seem to stop herself. "*This* must be the fun part," she said, unsuccessfully squelching a chuckle.

He blew the match out an instant before it could singe his fingertips. His warm breath touched Kyla's cheek, lifted the hair at her temples, fanned a new sensation to life. She could see nothing away from the firelight but she knew exactly where he was as his hands settled on her hips. The hard length of his body pressed against her, welding her back and shoulders to the wall.

"No, this is the fun part," he whispered. His lips brushed hers, testing the acceptance of the mouth quivering under his. With a gentle nuzzling, he coaxed her lips apart to tongue the delicate edges of her teeth. That sizzle ripped through her again, and her responding gasp offered up the intimacy of her mouth. Then she was tasting his tongue as he thoroughly explored the satin flesh of her mouth.

A wave of longing washed over her, sweeping her mind free of thought, except for one—that it seemed the most appropriate way to end an utterly reckless day, running headlong into an equally reckless kiss.

Two

The dark was solid, engulfing, thick enough to touch. With sight obliterated, Kyla's other senses grew acute. Luke's breath thundered past her ear, swirled on her skin. His mouth tasted of sweet, sweet intimacy. From the collar of his shirt drifted the scent of male skin bathed in musky after-shave. Wherever he touched her he left his brand: with the stamp of his body pressed from her knees to her shoulders; and the imprint of his hands at her waist, sliding down her thighs, cupping her bottom to bring them closer.

"Now, this is good," Luke muttered at her open mouth. "Ah, love, it's the best."

Kyla sighed. "Oh, Luke." Her hands closed convulsively on the bunched muscles of his arms. "This is crazy . . . no more."

But his tongue touched the words, swept them from her mouth, dipping between her lips with a tenderness that squeezed her heart. Seconds later she relaxed enough to stroke his tongue with hers, feeling its exquisite texture, discovering its abilities.

"I've wanted to do this from the first moment you turned at that window," Luke murmured. "From the second I laid eyes on you."

Kyla believed him, remembering how unsteadily she had reeled with the same intoxication. There had been disquieting sparks in the green eyes, warning her to keep her distance. And later, fascination for him had glued her to the back step of Pop's store and prodded her to visually lap him up.

"And now you have." Her voice sounded loud to her own ears. And decisive, thank goodness! She wished she could see his face, but her eyes opened to a hazy darkness. "It's time . . . I started dinner. The . . . generator?"

He obediently withdrew. A rush of cool air insulted her body where he had blanketed her with warmth. She heard the irritating scratch of another match. The light seared her eyes, an orange glow painfully stabbing at her dilated pupils. Luke held the flaming tip close to her face and Kyla wondered what he could see, staring so intently at her.

Did he see the pounding pulse in the veins at her temples? Was awakened desire pleading silently in her eyes? Could he distinguish between the natural fullness of her lips and the swelling caused by the tender suction of his kiss?

Whatever he saw, it brought a smile to his lips and Kyla found her gaze riveted to his perfectly sculptured mouth. "The generator," she forced from a dry throat as the second match burned to his fingertips.

A short time later, with the electricity restored thanks to a replaced spark plug, Kyla stood near Luke at the kitchen counter. Grateful for a simple task, she arranged the steak on a broiling pan and popped it under the flames while he lathered engine grease from his hands at the sink. As he was drying them off Kyla noticed how gingerly he ran the terrycloth towel through his fingers.

"Luke?" She tugged the dish towel from his hands. "Did you hurt yourself?"

"No . . . I'm fine, Kyla." He let her turn his palms up for inspection. When she probed at the raised blisters, he sucked air between his teeth. She threw a questioning look at him as he tried to pull his hands free.

"How did you get these?"

A negligent shrug accompanied his answer. "It's been the better part of a year since I've manhandled an ax. They'll be fine tomorrow, Kyla."

"They'll be nasty sores tomorrow. There's a first-aid ointment in the medicine chest. Wait here, I'll get it."

"Kyla . . ." But she was already off to the bathroom, disrupting the shelves behind the mirrored doors. When Kyla returned she squeezed a generous dab of balm on his welted palms. "That's too much," Luke protested. "I won't be able to keep a grip on anything all night."

"Lucky me." Kyla chuckled. "And to think *you* called *me* a tenderfoot. Hah!" Kyla forced herself to concentrate as she massaged the clear jelly over the pads and hollows of his palms. Her fingers slid easily over his flesh, the ointment a slick lubricant. It took all her self-control not to include his wrists or venture to touch the crisp hairs sprinkled over his forearms beneath his sleeves.

"Any other repercussions of your day pretending to be Mr. Mountain Man?"

"Mm-hmm. I'm sore all over."

Kyla slapped the ointment tube into his hand. "My gift. Take it home with you."

"But who will rub it on my aching back? I could strip now and you could—"

"No," Kyla murmured. A picture formed in her mind, leaving her bones as unsteady as hot liquid. His arms slipped around her when she swayed. Then her chin was cupped in his lotion-soft palm and her face tipped up. His hand at her back moved up her spine, lifting the heavy hair at her neck. He dropped his head and nuzzled her throat with open mouth and flicking tongue.

"No," she gasped. "It . . . burn . . ."

"Mmm . . . yes. *Burn*, Kyla."

"No . . . it . . . it will burn . . . the steak." She worked herself free, the flat of her hands spread on his chest. "I have to turn the steak over."

He crossed his arms at his chest, quietly watching her make the final dinner preparations. "I'm going too fast for you."

"You noticed that, did you?" Anger at her own appalling abandonment sharpened her retort. Attraction to the man, normal in any healthy woman, was growing into more than visual appreciation. And that was dangerous, she knew.

"Want me to slow down? We've got a whole week, after all." Kyla nearly dropped the china serving platter.

"Here, let me have that." He neatly removed the plate from her doubtful grip before the steak could fall to the floor. "I may have to leave here hungry tonight. I don't want to be starving as well."

Kyla blew out an exasperated breath, aiming it at the supple male body ambling out of the kitchen. How the hell was she going to handle him? She couldn't even handle herself! He was the sexiest, most magnificent man she had ever met. He dominated her rooms, provoked her body, and obliterated her judgment.

And he wanted her.

Kyla tore her thoughts away from what it would be like to give him what he wanted. Forcing herself to function, she picked up the salad bowl and directed her feet to the living room. The matched lamps flanking the sofa had been turned off and Luke had added a pair of tall candles to the table. The walls blushed with firelight and reflections of flame danced on the ceiling. Subtler, maybe, she thought—not slower.

When Luke held her chair out, Kyla hesitated. Suddenly she knew she had to send him home this very second. To let him stay was to cross another invisible line into alien territory. For the second time that day Kyla knew a strong urge to bolt.

"Put 'er down, Kyla," he ordered softly. She sank into the chair, her eyes level with the stitching on his trouser pocket. He didn't move and her eyes slid up his towering length to find him staring down at her.

"My Lord, you really are a little thing . . . almost *too* small."

She ground her teeth together as anger flashed through her, superseding the anxious thoughts of a moment ago. He let his hand drift from the chair back to brush her shoulder before he finally stepped around the table and took the seat across from her.

"If you dare say you could tuck me in your pocket, I will ram my size-five foot through it and prove what a ridiculous statement that is. Why does it never occur to people that observations like that are not cute compliments?" Kyla snapped her napkin in the air before shoving it onto her lap. "And what if I said it's *you* who are too *big*! How does that make you feel?"

"Worried," Luke murmured. "In the last hour it's occurred to me that I *am* too big . . . for you."

Oh, he was impossible! "What you're too big for is your own britches."

Laughter tumbled from him as amused agreement sparkled in his eyes.

"I . . . I meant your ego."

"My ego isn't in my britches."

Kyla coolly cocked a brow at him. "Oh, no? Could have fooled me."

"My, my, but your size is a sore spot. Created problems for you, has it?"

"From day one!"

"Daddy's little girl?"

Kyla nodded. "Mom's too. It didn't help that I arrived in this world weighing less than five pounds." Curious, the way he'd smoothly subverted her anger. "It didn't help either that I followed three strapping brothers. I suppose I scared them, being so little after a trio of quarterbacks."

"Three brothers should have toughened you up."

"Not if they valued their lives. If they so much as bumped me in passing, my father came roaring out of his recliner chair like a lion from his den. I didn't dare join in their backyard games. According to my mother, male-inflicted injuries would leave me lame, maimed, or barren."

"Is that how she put it?"

"Put what?"

"Making love. A male-inflicted injury?" Kyla sputtered, choking on a piece of steak. "You're practically inhaling dinner. Do you always eat so much?" He tipped his head thoughtfully. "It was a courageous decision for you to come to the mountains alone, wasn't it?"

Another swift change of subject. At least this one was safer. "I do experience spurts of courage, although they're few and far between. My last was two years ago. Surfing. I came to on the sand with a burly lifeguard doing push-ups on my chest until I made him happy by spewing out a gallon of salt water. I had a concussion, a broken ankle, and the skin on the left side of my body had been sandblasted away." Kyla watched the uncertain flicker of the candle flame, grimacing at the memory. "I'm not a very physical person."

"Are you a married person?" Luke asked quietly.

Such a relevant question, reserved until now and so perfunctorily asked between a bite of garlic bread and a sip of wine, struck Kyla as preposterous, and she laughed. "Would it make any difference to you?"

"Are you married, Kyla?"

He released a held breath at her quiet "No."

Was *he*? she wondered. If the possibility of her having a husband hadn't discouraged his advances, was it likely a wife would be any deterrent? He was not a man who went long without a woman, Kyla was sure of that. But a wife? A woman entitled to more than a night in this man's bed? A woman who shared his home, his name, his children? It was abhorrent to her.

"Are *you* married?"

"No." His hand covered hers on the table, his thumb rubbing her wrist until her pulse leapt wildly. "Lovers?"

"Plural? As in two or three or twenty?" *He wasn't married*, she thought with relief.

"Any?"

"Not at the moment." Kyla took a healthy gulp of wine, then swirled the long-stemmed tulip glass, watching the candlelight fracture on the undulating golden surface. "And I plan to keep it that way."

"Forever?"

"For the time being."

"Then if an emotional upheaval didn't drive you to these mountains, what did?"

"A Jaguar," Kyla bantered, already wishing she hadn't been so easy to extract information from. Her personal life, her sexual activity, were none of his business. What was wrong with her anyway? Here she was envying the nonexistent wife of a perfect stranger!

Kyla eased her hand out from under his. She poured coffee for both of them, intently ignoring his pensive gaze.

"Intriguing," Luke murmured.

The way he said it rankled. As if she were playing at being coy, weaving a web of mystery into which he was supposed to be lured and eventually trapped. That wasn't her style, but she certainly wasn't going to disprove it by confiding in him when she didn't want to.

Who was he anyway? Obviously not the handyman she had first assumed. His hands, while not baby-soft, were free of calluses. She had noticed, when applying the ointment, that his fingernails were meticulously clean and manicured. He did not have the hands of a laborer. Or the bent carriage. Or the lumbering gait.

"Enough about me," she said. "Tell me about you. I assumed you worked for Pop. Do you live up here?"

"No. I live in Los Angeles." He smiled at her raised eyebrows. "Ah, a *civilized* man, she says to herself."

"I never doubted you were civilized, Luke."

"Like hell! I scared the wits out of you this afternoon." He laughed gently. "You reminded me of a startled doe with big velvet eyes staring at a hunter before loping off to safety."

"But I didn't lope off at all."

"No. You were a brave girl, puffing out your lovely chest with pretend bravado. I took great pains to look every bit the gentleman tonight."

Her hand went to the part of her anatomy he had complimented. Why didn't she send him away? "Who are you?" she asked. "I mean, what do you do? In Los Angeles. And why aren't you there doing it now?"

"In the civilian world I am a man in transition. Up here I'm a dutiful son checking on his parents' cabin. I had this afternoon free to help my friend Jake."

His green eyes fastened on her features as if to say: I can be a mystery too. But Kyla had been in the business world long enough to know that a man who said he was "in transition," and was in the mountains midweek, was a man without a job. She was dying to ask his field. Further questions, however, would only spotlight his unemployment, she decided.

"Well, don't we make a fine pair," she said lightly. "A man in transition and an intriguing woman."

"A phenomenal pair."

That voice! That voice could melt Alaska! she marveled. Her right leg, crossed over her left knee, met and remet the relaxed muscles of his calf under the table. Clothed though it was, each contact sent on electric jolt through her. It was time for distance, breathing space, thinking room. Kyla stood up and, hugging her arms to her, walked to the wall of picture windows. On a night like this, without the moon's silvery illumination or its imprint on the lake's surface, the windows were inky mirrors of the room. There was nothing beyond the glass at all.

"Not a single lit cabin." Kyla spoke the thought aloud. "Isn't anyone up here, Luke?"

"Probably not. We'll get a few people on the weekend."

She watched his image in the glass as he left the table to poke at the fire. He fed a fresh log to the flames, filling the room with snaps and hisses as juicy sap simmered. The windows were selective mirrors. The furniture, the walls, the throw rugs, failed to exist. Only the flickering candle glow and the roaring fire danced on the ebony surface. And she and Luke, bathed in firelight, were moving around as if in a cave. Was she really that softly pretty? she wondered. Or had the vague reflection blurred the definite shape of her nose and chin and melted years away from her features?

Luke crossed to the bar and poured a cognac, only one. Kyla watched his reflection come to her, stand behind her, offer the snifter to her. She accepted it and her eyes dropped to the duplicated image of his foot, fitted so close to her strappy sandal. She studied them as they appeared on the window. He stood behind and to the side of her, her soft skirt hem clinging to his slacks below his knee. His hand . . . Her mouth went dry as she looked at his hand splayed over her midriff, his thumb at the hollow between her breasts, his middle finger tracking her belt, his little finger pointing down and pressing on the soft flesh beneath her stomach. She lifted her eyes, past her own face, to his square chin, resting on the top of her head. To his eyes. He had been watching her watching them.

"My love, I could hurt you without meaning to. That scares me."

Kyla took a sip of cognac, hoping it would burn off the cloud of sensuality enveloping her brain.

"How is it?" he murmured.

"How is . . . what?"

"Your brandy."

"Oh. Sharp. No, sweet . . . uh . . ."

"Let me taste." She tried to raise the glass but his thumb and finger circling her wrist stopped her. "Open your mouth, Kyla. Let me taste."

Her response was ungoverned by thought. Even as her hands desperately gripped the snifter she turned her head on his chest and tipped her face up to him. Her lips separated and her eyelids grew heavy, almost closing as she melted into the moment. Through the fan of her lashes she watched his tongue seek her mouth. He licked the sticky residue from her lips, taking the taste into his own mouth to savor.

"Delicious . . . very sweet." He rubbed her chin with his thumb as he kissed her again. He searched for brandy from every droplet in her mouth until she had only the flavor of herself to offer him. Her legs began to weaken. Luke caught her behind her knees and lifted her into his arms. He carried her only as far as the sofa, where he sat with her in his lap, gently removing the snifter from her hands.

He was immobilizing her head for another kiss when she tried to push away from him. The refusal she was about to voice came across loud and clear in her russet eyes.

"Don't be frightened," Luke mumbled into her hair. "I'll stop wherever and whenever you ask me to."

"Then stop here and now," Kyla begged in an urgent whisper.

He slid his face over her hair until his eyes met hers. "I have to start before I can stop."

"No, Luke—"

"Yes, Kyla, yes." And he molded his mouth to hers again. His feet came off the floor to rest on the edge of a low table in front of the sofa, as he further nestled Kyla into his lap.

Her fingertips lay at the base of his neck and, seeking, Kyla moved them over his face, brailling his prominent cheekbones, the soft hollow beneath. She touched a crease in his forehead and traced it to where it disappeared into his hairline. Plunging into the glorious silk, she raked her fingers over his scalp to his neck, delighting in the way she ruffled through, unhindered by a tangle.

His deft fingers made child's play of her blouse buttons. Then the soft caress of fire-warmed air kissed her exposed skin. His palms swept over her bared midriff and lacy bra to cover the pulsing cord in her throat. The warmth of his hand at her neck washed through her veins like a simmering flood.

"My hands are so raw right now," Luke muttered hoarsely. "So sensitive, I can feel every detail of your skin. Here velvet, here satin. And soft, so soft." Her nylon-sheathed leg knew the touch of his hand; then his fingers slipped between stockings and heel strap and each shoe in turn was dropped to the floor. His powerful hand kneaded her feet and massaged her arches, the muscle-soothing waves coursing all the way to her shoulders.

"You feel so good, Kyla," he murmured, his lips embracing the pale swell of breast above her bra. "A sweet morsel for slow savoring."

Then his hand covered her breast, his fingers tenderly manipulating the rigid bud of her nipple. Her blood, flowing like molten lava, turned to ice water; her spine went rigid as a steel rod. "Luke, this is . . . crazy," she gasped out, straining now, with her hands flat against his sweatered chest, to push herself away from him. "We're . . . strangers."

"Relax," he crooned. "Relax, love."

"Oh, no. Relax tonight, regret tomorrow."

His golden head came up and eyes bright with passion searched her face. "I want you, Kyla. You want me."

She moved off his lap, shaking her head. "No, I don't." But she did, and it scared the hell out of her. Her blouse was open, his eyes riveted to the provocative lingerie that hid so little, she might have been naked.

"You can't lie, love. I see how much you need me."

She closed her blouse with shaky hands and nodded. "But that's physical, Luke. I have to have more than that. Please, don't insist. Let me go."

"And if I don't?"

"If you don't, I'll soon find myself in bed with you . . . too soon."

"But willing, Kyla."

"Willing. Oh, Lord." Speech strangled in her throat as she envisioned his lean, supple body, unclothed and ministering to her. "Willing," she breathed. "And tomorrow I'd hate both of us. Because what's going on here just isn't something I approve of."

She turned away from his burning gaze and buttoned her blouse. Her skirt was hiked up on her legs and she tugged the hem down, all the while feeling the weight of his eyes on her. She waited, tensed, for his reaction. He had every right to erupt with rage, to release his engorged passion in some sort of angry outburst. She had known from the beginning she wouldn't go to bed with him.

"You need more?" He feathered her lips with his own, sending regret as well as desire racing through her. "What? Tell me, I'll give it to you."

"It isn't something asked for or given. It grows, Luke. It becomes."

He raked his fingers through his tousled hair. A deep breath brought some control to his quaking body. Then his gentle arms gathered her up in a non-sexual but utterly sensuous embrace.

"I don't want you to hate us. I said I'd slow down and I will. I will, love."

Kyla concentrated on the relief she felt, having cleared that hurdle, and tried to forget how exhausting her vacation might be if Luke Hudson decided to spend *his* vacation seducing her.

"You have to go now." Kyla walked to the door, feeling him behind her. "Uh, Luke?" She stopped him on the threshold. "Did you mean it about grizzlies and coyotes?"

"Mm-hmm. If you need me, love, just whistle." His voice was smooth as cream, and just as silky. "You do know how to whistle, don't you?"

Oh, he can't be serious! she thought.

"Just put your lips together." He smiled. "Curl your tongue, insert two fingers, and . . ." He then let go a whistle so shrill Kyla jumped and her eyes popped wide open. "I live clear across the lake."

Later that night she convinced herself that Luke had nothing to do with the twisted sheets and her unanswered prayers for the oblivion of sleep.

Maybe Susie Barrett, CompuMart's receptionist, had extrasensory powers after all. "You won't sleep nights if you go away and leave Brad Upton here this week," she had warned Kyla. "He'll pull some razzle-dazzle deal out of his hat and, presto, instant veep. Mark my words, you won't sleep a wink."

Was Kyla naive to believe her record would speak for her if she weren't there to do it for herself? It was cruel fate that she'd scheduled her vacation to fall at this particular time. She had considered putting it off, but Lord, it had been a difficult year and the strain in the office once the vice-presidency had opened up had only increased Kyla's need to get away.

Besides, she didn't really believe Brad Upton would get the promotion. Razzle-dazzle had its place, and the vice-president's office wasn't it.

Kyla punched her pillow into a fluffier headrest. Would Chuck Myers take advantage of her absence? She shouldn't have left. She should have stayed in L.A. and closed the deal with that new client, introduced a new software line to one of her key accounts.

"Andrew is a fair man," she reminded the darkness. "He'll make the choice that's best for CompuMart."

Kyla remembered how fair he'd been to her when she'd first applied for a job five years ago, a Chicago transplant who had spent her last dollar making the move to California. When he had asked for a reference her first instinct had been to lie, to say she'd spent the last few years nursing a sick parent or that she'd worked for one of her brothers, and hope one would stick up for her if called. But she couldn't. She'd already lost so much; trading her self-respect for employment would have left her empty.

And so, with a deep breath and a voice devoid of emotion, she'd given an overview of her years as a distributor of medical equipment. Harder to explain was why Zachary Fullerton had fired her when she was so damn good at sales.

Zach, to whom she'd given herself and been destroyed by in return. Zach, who had taken her as a lover and then cold-bloodedly demolished her career. She'd fallen in love with her boss, become engaged to him, and then been fired because it was against company policy—his policy—for a husband and wife to work together. Besides, he'd said to her stunned face, she wasn't going to work after they were married. She wasn't?

When she'd given him back his ring he'd been

furious, suffering a wounded ego more than a broken heart. Wherever she applied for work in the weeks that followed she was enthusiastically greeted, until they checked her references. Kyla was at a loss to understand the slamming doors until, finally, faced with her tears of frustration, one man told her what Zach said to all who called him: that she'd been fired for sleeping her way to the top. Without being able to deny her affair with Zach, she had no defense left.

Andrew Carson had listened and then, instead of calling Zach, he'd contacted her past clients. He'd liked what he heard, enough to hire her.

Andrew Carson was a fair man. Kyla hugged that thought to herself. It was lonely comfort, as all comforts had been since Zach. There hadn't been a man in her life since, until . . . Until? Where had that come from? Until when? Tonight? Until who? Luke? No, Luke Hudson was not in her life. He'd barely been in her living room three hours. She didn't have room for him or anyone else right now; Chuck Myers and Brad Upton were already a crowd.

She turned from stomach to back, looking for a comfortable sleeping position. *Oh, Kyla, it's useless,* she thought desperately. She figured the sun would come up to find her still sorting them all out. Brad and Chuck, Andrew Carson, Zach Fullerton and Luke Hudson. For a woman without a man in her life, there were a helluva lot of men in her life.

And yet, when she woke in a room illuminated by the vague light of a sun filtered through a leafy umbrella, Kyla felt rested and refreshed. The fire in the living room had died during the night and the chilly air that filled the cottage had helped the few hours of sleep to be deep, restorative ones.

She made a pot of coffee and took a steaming mug out to the patio, snug and warm in a sweatsuit. The night's chill still lingered and she found the crisp mountain air invigorating. After her usual warm-up exercises, Kyla went down to the lake path for her morning run, a daily ritual to combat the hours spent behind a desk. The tree limbs and irregular ruts in the path made it too dangerous for jogging, so she settled for a brisk walk instead.

Hearing a splash, Kyla veered off onto a short wooden dock precariously propped over the water on decaying piles. Sinewy arms ripped through the lake's glassy surface and she recognized Luke's blond head as he stopped to grab a breath and rest. His shucked-off jeans, yellow T-shirt, and rope sandals lay in a heap at the end of the tilted dock and Kyla sat down next to the pile, dangling her feet a few inches from the water.

Luke turned in the middle of the lake and swam back. He snapped his head to the side, clearing his eyes of water and sending silver droplets in an airy arc. " 'Morning, Kyla. Sleep well?"

She grinned. "Super."

"If you didn't look so bright-eyed, I'd call you a liar. I didn't sleep worth a damn. Now, why don't you turn around and show me your cute little butt. It's cold in here." His teeth chattered as he trod water near her swinging feet. "Duck back in those trees and let me out."

"So modest! I wouldn't have thought it of you, Luke. Having grown up with three brothers means I'm rarely embarrassed by a man's state of dress. But if it bothers you, I'll turn my head."

"Won't bother me a bit."

Her three brothers, all getting ready at once for Saturday-night dates in a house with only one bathroom, had accustomed Kyla to male legs and torsos sprouting from any manner of brief male attire. They were all just another pair of pants to Kyla.

Luke disappeared around the side of the dock where a ladder to the surface had been crudely constructed. She saw his hands reach up from below and wrap around the top rung to haul his dripping head and shoulders up. Another rung and his chest and tapering waist came into view. The blond hairs narrowing down to his navel were drenched to dark brown. Kyla had every intention of turning her eyes away at the first sight of wet elastic hugging his hips. He took another lunging step and the wetly plastered hairs widened back out again.

"Oh, my Lord!" He was stark naked! Kyla scrambled to her feet, spinning away from the shock of it and groaning through clenched teeth, "Oh, damn!"

"I thought you couldn't be embarrassed," Luke said to her back when he had stopped laughing.

"I didn't say I couldn't be. Just that it was rare. Why didn't you say something?"

"I think I did. In fact, I'm sure of it."

"Where's your underwear, for goodness' sake?"

"Rarely wear it. A redundant piece of clothing."

"Oh, Luke," Kyla moaned.

"You can turn around, love. I'm decent."

When she did turn back she didn't see him in the clothes that clung in damp patches to his wet body. Instead she still saw the magnificent bronzed nude that had glistened in the morning sun.

Three

Kyla stamped her foot, causing a tremor in the rotting deck. Lord, her responses to him were becoming more adolescent by the moment. But he had to know that his stepping naked from the water would embarrass her. How dare he humiliate her when it could have easily been avoided? she thought angrily.

"Damn you! Why did you do that?" Somehow the words struggled past the lump in her throat.

"I was cold." Luke strode toward her. Before Kyla could jump back he had taken her by the arm and pulled her to the lake path. "I wanted to get out. And why are you so hot under the collar? I'm the one caught with his pants down . . . or off, as the case may be."

Kyla bristled with fury. The man had demeaned her, and she didn't like it one bit. The psychological upper hand was her strength and it rankled when a man bested her. Gathering her shattered dignity, she squared her shoulders and leveled her tone. "That's precisely the point. A simple explanation would have sufficed. Instead you . . . you—"

"Accelerated this process of you getting to know me better. Keeping in mind how cold that water—"

"Oh, shut up!"

Kyla wrenched her arm free and stalked off alone. A hundred angry paces into the woods she came to a halt and ground her fists at her eye sockets, trying to wipe out the stubborn image of Luke, naked and magnificent. *Despite the cold water,* her subconscious mind added.

She set off again, wildly batting away branches. "I could be, *should* be, on a sandy beach with civilized strangers who wouldn't dare come prancing naked from the surf." The heat of a furious flush struck an additional blow to her pride. Why, she hadn't blushed since . . . since Luke had fondled her slip. But before that it had been at least ten years! And stamping her foot! The man had the most aggravating way of reducing her behavior to that of a teenager.

She was behaving as though she'd never seen a naked man before. Unexpectedly, a low-pitched moan filtered through her clenched teeth. What she hadn't seen before were shoulders that might have been molded by Michelangelo, the flat belly and tight buttocks of a man in extraordinary physical condition, and lean, powerful legs dusted with gold fur. From the top of his head to the tip of his toes, Luke Hudson was solid bronze, with no white skin to proclaim the modesty of a bathing suit. Utter masculine beauty, she admitted shakily, and unforgettable.

An hour later, after Kyla had indulged her abraded nerves with a feast of bacon and eggs and the last of the coffee, there came a heavy knock at her door. Lifting ruffled curtains, she peered out. Luke. He was dressed, but even so her heart began tripping over itself. A fishing rod rested on his shoulder, the straps of a bulging canvas pack crossed his chest over his yellow shirt, and a picnic hamper sat near his feet.

"Now what?" Kyla demanded after flinging open

the door. "If I'd wanted to be hounded all week by a watchdog, I'd have brought a Saint Bernard with me."

"Got to move this archaic getting-acquainted ritual along. Surface impressions are fine, but I'd like to be wanted for more than my body. We're going to a favorite haunt of my childhood so you can pick my brain. I'll answer any questions you think you need to ask a prospective lover."

She ignored the last part of his declaration, but found it hard to ignore the blood climbing up her neck because of it. "You owe me an apology."

"For what? You were given a rare treat, my girl. Not many people are privileged to see me in the buff."

The appearance of his boyish dimple assuaged some of her anger. And he *was* offering her an alternative to sitting around the cabin all day with little to do. "But I've never been fishing, Luke. I'll be a lousy companion."

"I'll do the fishing; you'll be busy asking questions. Change first, long sleeves and slacks."

"But it's getting hot!" Kyla had exchanged her sweatsuit for shorts and a tube top in deference to the climbing temperature.

"We're going to a special place, not the lake. I'd hate like hell to have to keep my distance because your delicate skin is scratched. Move it, love, time's a-wasting."

Wearing a long-sleeved blue cotton blouse and sturdy jeans, Kyla trailed after Luke along a path that eventually tapered off into a narrow rut, then disappeared completely. Luke held branches back, hauled her over fallen trunks, and tugged her through prickly thickets that snagged at her clothes. Then Kyla heard a sound reminiscent of static from an untuned radio. After the woodpecker incident, she decided to refrain from voicing her observation.

"Hear the rapids?" Luke said.

"Of course, rapids!" She glanced up and met his quizzical expression. "Radio static . . ."

"Static." He shook his head in disbelief. "Do us both a favor, tenderfoot, and don't get it into your head to go off exploring on your own."

A few more yards and the leafy surroundings fell away. Cottony clouds drifted in a bright blue sky and the sun at high noon shimmered on the fast-moving stream. The water was shallow and clean and the stone-pebbled riverbed was occasionally visible through the rushing water.

Luke dragged an old blanket out of the backpack and spread it on a spongy patch of moss. He opened two beers from the cooler and handed one to Kyla. She gulped it gratefully while scanning the paraphernalia in his tackle box. Cubbyholes were filled with shiny disks, colorful feathers, and painstakingly detailed miniatures of fish.

"If you squint your eyes and let it blur out of focus it could be a jewelry case." Kyla chose an elaborate lure and dangled it at her earlobe, playfully batting her eyes at Luke.

Like a proud mountain lion sprawled for a sunbath, Luke stretched out on a tabletop boulder, his back resting at the massive trunk of a Douglas fir. He lit a cigarette, took a swig of beer, and smiled.

"You look like you own the joint, Luke."

"I've been sitting on this rock, fishing this stream, as far back as I can remember. See here? How it's rounded out and worn down? My rock. It fits me well."

Kyla lay on the blanket, turned her face up to the sun, and closed her eyes. The grit of his baritone voice rasped along her senses, sending messages to her brain that had nothing to do with what he was saying.

"Did you come to the mountains often as a little boy?" she asked, wanting the voice as much as the answer.

"Mm-hmm. The day school let out for the summer, Mom, Dad, and I packed up and moved to the cabin until school resumed in the fall."

"You were an only child?"

"Mm-hmm."

"Your father didn't have to work?"

"He taught high-school math and auto mechanics. While his colleagues worked odd jobs in the summer months teaching summer school and tutoring, my father invented in a small workshop he built onto the back of our cabin."

"Would I know any of his inventions?"

"No." Sadness lowered his voice and Kyla was surprised to find she knew him well enough to sense it. "He patented a few of them, but nothing ever panned out. What he had when he was finished was very crude. Patent searches are expensive, patents even more so. He didn't have adequate funds to find and get commitments from backers. The capital to market a product himself was far beyond his reach."

Some of the computer lines Kyla handled had started as crude models of men's dreams, patched together in a garage or basement. "It must have been a terrible disappointment for him."

"Yes"—now she heard a smile in his voice—"but he's a stubborn old coot. He's retired now. And still inventing."

A rustle in the undergrowth bolted Kyla to a sitting position and her eyes snapped open. "What's that?" she blurted.

Luke started laughing. In the way of a true Californian, he dug a hole in the ground with his heel and buried his smoked cigarette, kicking damp earth over the ash to prevent a fire. "Something tiny and harmless. A squirrel, or maybe a chipmunk. You are a skittish city girl, aren't you?"

"I have no desire to meet up with one of your grizzlies." Kyla lay back down. Timidly, her dark eyes investigated her surroundings. Vivid little flowers poked through the undergrowth and birds pranced up and down the leafy boughs overhead. Not only was everything harmless, she decided, but so heavenly peaceful too. Then the sun's glare was blocked as Luke came to her, his body poised, suspended above her. A breath caught halfway between her lips and her lungs. On impulse, she raised her arms and put her hands on his shoulders, not to push him away, not to pull him closer—but to touch him, just to touch him.

"Luke?" A hundred uncertainties wavered in her voice.

"I'm a manageable beast, Kyla, remember? No need to be frightened of me." His eyes were drawn to her breasts, which suddenly heaved as she grabbed an overdue breath. With his hands framing her face, his thumbs gliding along her cheekbones, he sank to his elbows. When her breasts met his chest, a near-silent moan was expelled with his breath.

With incredible gentleness he placed his lips on hers, and not for the first time, it occurred to Kyla to be very frightened. As the kiss deepened, the strength in his arms ebbed. Kyla eagerly absorbed the weight of him. Their legs tangled together. The moss under the blanket cushioned the burden of his body, and the softness of her thighs cushioned his arousal.

"You look so right here," Luke murmured. "So wild and untamed."

"That's just my hair. It *is* wild. But not the rest of me. I'm a tenderfoot, Luke." He wasn't the sort of man a woman made love with, then blithely walked away from. Kyla felt she couldn't afford the risk of emotional upheaval right now—not with the promotion so close, the hours of commitment it would demand.

"Don't talk." Another uninhibited moan burst from his throat. He released the trembling sound into her mouth and it echoed in her soul. He circled her slim waist with both hands, his thumbs and fingers nearly touching. "Such a fragile flower. You make me feel clumsy. And much too big."

But he was all gentleness and grace to Kyla. A haze of passion clouded her judgment of a moment ago and she flirted with danger. With shaky hands she opened the buttons of his shirt, impatiently shoving the material aside. Her fingers tangled in crinkly blond fur, kneaded his flesh, relished the supple bronzed skin covering hard muscle.

"Yes, Kyla. Touch me, love."

His urgent plea was a torch burning through the fog. It was not the contours of his chest he begged her to touch, nor the aroused nubs of his nipples. He wanted her boldest, fiercest grasp. Her hands stilled and she struggled to catch her breath. His tongue traced a light blue vein from her small chin to the deep opening of her blouse. *Oh, Lord,* she moaned silently. She seemed only able to stop herself, never to stop him.

Luke touched her over her clothes, trying to coax from her the caress he so desired. When it wasn't forthcoming, he grew still and groaned. "I've got to get my mind on other things and my hands off you, or go crazy." His gaze showered her with warmth and understanding. "And so gorgeous too. Okay, we'll hide it. That's it. Ugly you up a bit."

"Mmm . . . what?"

Kyla felt him slowly uncoil. He rolled to his side and tugged the backpack closer.

Kyla looked Luke up and down. "Definitely ugly."

Black rubber waders waterproofed his legs from his toes to the top of his muscled thighs; a hunter's green vest with small Velcro-closure pockets hung on his shoulders, and a brimmed hat dangling ornamental fish hid his thick blond mane. Kyla was outfitted in like attire and her tumble of hair was tucked under an identical hat. She had no intention of digging into one single pocket to discover the oddities contained there.

"You're a good sport, Kyla." He extended a hand from the bank to lead her into the stream. "Take it slow. Get a feel for the current and step carefully. The rocks can be slippery."

Kyla clamped onto his wrist with both hands. She was momentarily unbalanced by the tug of swift water at her ankles, at her knees. When she reached the middle, where it was thigh-deep, she was better able to judge the speed and direction of the flood and compensate by leaning into it. Luke inched upstream from her and Kyla watched him swing his rod in the air, reacquainting his hand to the grip.

"First lesson in fly-casting coming up."

"Uh-uh. You're fishing, I'm picking your brain. Remember?"

"Are you sure you have three brothers?"

"Positive, and they treated me like a breakable doll, placing me on a throne at the sidelines. I told you, Luke, I never dirtied my pretty pink dresses. Never skinned my knees or climbed a tree."

"Then it's about time you learned to fish." He curled her reluctant fingers around the rod grip. "Stretch your arm out like this. Good. Then swing . . . snap." Four feet of line plopped out in front of her. "Not bad. Try again."

"Oh, Luke. I've seen *The American Sportsman* on TV. The line is supposed to release and snake through the air and land in the next state. Not at my knees."

"Here, watch me." Luke illustrated expert casting. Seconds after the feathery lure touched down, he executed some fancy arm action and the silver cord was lacing the air to land yards away behind him. "You want to simulate a grasshopper skipping over the water. Or you can let it lie there awhile like a fish fly. Do you know what a fish fly is?"

"Ugh, yes. We don't have them in Chicago, but we

vacationed in Michigan once and the smelly things were everywhere."

"Chicago. When did you move to California?"

"Five years ago."

"What were you doing in Chicago five years ago?"

Kyla had bravely wandered away from him and was studying a large fish hiding in the quiet waters at the base of a submerged log. It would probably be the height of poor taste, she decided, just to reach down and grab it up in her hands when Luke was proudly pitting human limitations against nature to get one in such macho fashion.

"Kyla, I asked what you did in Chicago."

She looked over her shoulder at him. "Besides live there? I was in sales at MSD—Medical Systems Distributors. Marketing high-tech diagnostic equipment to hospitals and clinics."

Luke threw his head back and laughed. "That's rich. So you found a way to go out and play hardball with the big boys after all."

Kyla frowned. She'd never thought of her career choice as an entrance to the male world she'd always been forbidden. Was it? Lord knew her mother had repeated her rules of appropriate behavior for little girls and young women for Kyla's first eighteen years, effectively squelching her ambitions. And it was true that she competed with men on a daily basis now. Kyla was too delicately built to best a man on a physical level, but she had to admit to feeling great satisfaction when she bested one on a profit-and-loss statement.

"And what do you do now?" Luke interrupted her disquieting thoughts.

"Same thing." Selling was selling; it made no difference to Kyla what the product was. "Only now I'm a regional manager dealing in bulk sales to outlets, no end-users."

Luke whistled. "Very impressive. Now, come back here and impress me with your fly casting."

Kyla winked at the glassy-eyed fish peeking out from the rock and then trudged back to Luke. The rod felt less unwieldy in her hand. She developed a certain rhythm, whipping it out, pulling it back. Then she tried to backlash the line, but it didn't respond. Thinking she was caught on a rock or sunken log, Kyla took a few ungainly steps forward. The line remained taut and the rod bowed in an arc with the tip pointing at the water.

In a splashing sparkle of silver spray, the big old fish leapt out of the water. "Luke, help! He's got me! What do I do?"

Luke was stunned, standing there with his mouth hanging open and the most surprised look in his eyes. Then he was plowing through the water to her side. "That must have been one hungry sucker for you to catch him," he complained. "Think aggressive. He doesn't have you—you've got him."

"Did I hear an editorial aside that it wasn't my skill that landed the big one?"

"Reel him in, smart aleck."

But she couldn't. The fish fought back with the strength of a whale. The whir of line spinning out followed each successful attempt of her prey to get the better of her. Luke finally took the rod and Kyla waded to the bank, soon to be joined by Luke with the netted fish.

"Rainbow trout. Six pounds if he's an ounce!" he announced. "Congratulations, tenderfoot."

Kyla stood mute as Luke laid the shimmery, flopping trout on the tabletop boulder. He worked gently at extracting the hook, careful not to rip through the mouth and gills. Her stomach shuddered crazily with each desperate slap of the powerful tail against the porous rock. He was literally drowning on air.

"Luke . . ."

"Look for my knife in my backpack, Kyla. I'll clean and bone him now, then put the fillets in the cooler.

You haven't tasted trout until I've grilled it. Melts in your mouth . . ."

"Luke . . ."

"A couple of baked potatoes wrapped in foil and roasted in the coals. A salad . . ."

"Luke . . ."

"Kyla, my pack, there behind you . . ." He finally looked up. At her face. At her eyes wide and fixed on the struggling fish. "Kyla? You all right?"

"I'm fine, Luke." Kyla smiled weakly. "Would you think I was crazy if I asked you to throw him back?"

"Throw him back? He's dinner."

"Please, before he dies?"

Luke sighed and rolled back to rest on his haunches. "Tell me why. I'm sure you've got a perfectly logical reason I haven't thought of."

"I really don't think I can eat him . . . now."

"Now? What do you mean, now?"

"He and I sort of met . . . over there by that log." Kyla looked at the slapping trout again. "Yes. I'm sure he's the one."

Luke groaned and shook his head. Kyla dropped to her knees and fastened dark, earnest eyes on him. His lips compressed to a firm line before a sigh of bewilderment separated them. "It's not as if the two of you shook hands and exchanged snapshots of the family. Oh, all right, love, I'll put him back. Damn those eyes of yours. I'll have to watch how you use them on me."

Luke scooped the trout up, cradling its thick center in cupped hands, and waded back into the stream. Kyla watched from the bank.

"It probably seems foolish . . ." she tried to explain.

"Definitely foolish."

"And a little stupid."

"A lot stupid." He eased his hands out from under the belly, freeing the fish.

"Thank you, Luke. Honest, I couldn't have eaten him."

The large iridescent body lay motionless, forced up against Luke's rubber-clad legs by the current. Then he struggled for a moment, not quite getting the swimming motion right. But, with a flap of his tail, he revived, and was carried out of sight by the current.

"Will he be okay?" Kyla asked, watching the water speed downstream. "He'll survive, won't he?"

"Maybe I should have taken him to the vet first?"

"I'm sorry, Luke. It's just so cold-blooded to me."

Luke peered down at her, unable to prevent the ends of his mouth from twitching up. "He'll be fine. If anything, we've given him a battle scar to flaunt for his friends. He'll probably tell some inflated tale about how *he* was the one to get away. All the girls will fall for it."

"I knew you'd understand."

"Tenderfoot, your wish is my command. Now, what do you want me to do about dinner?"

"No problem. I have this anonymous chicken in the freezer. I never met the poor soul. Didn't have to chase him around the yard to catch him. Didn't behead and pluck him. He'll taste delicious."

Luke playfully swiped the hat from her head, her tucked-up hair spilling in a liquid flame. "Let's get out of here, Kyla," he said huskily. "Now."

When they came out on the road Kyla relaxed in the relative civilization of a calm lake reflecting the afternoon sun. They had exited the woods just behind Pop's store and Luke asked if she'd mind their stopping to see how Jake was coming along with his Beth.

"Sure. See if they'd like some chicken soup from our leftovers. I can have it ready for their lunch tomorrow."

As they climbed the back step of Pop's house, her proposal drew Luke's green eyes to her upturned face

and the moment swelled with a new intimacy. "I will.
I'll ask him. You're a nice lady, Kyla Trent."

And he was a nice man, she thought. Very nice.
Kyla pretended interest in the door being opened and
greetings exchanged, but her mind was on Luke. A
devoted son who spoke with great love when he talked
of his father. And because of Luke, Pop would have
heat this winter. But there was so much she didn't
know—far too much for the kind of thoughts she was
thinking.

"We'd appreciate it, miss," Pop said to her when
Luke extended her offer of the soup. "But no need to
trouble yourself. You're up here on vacation and we
can't have you cooking for us."

"It's no trouble," Kyla said, and pressed the offer.

"Thank you, then. We'll accept." He smiled, some-
what abashedly. "My cooking . . ." His dramatic
wince wrinkled half his bald pate. "Awful. I do my best
but all we're tasting is the salt on the shoe leather."

Kyla and Luke departed, satisfied that, despite
Pop's cooking, Beth was in capable hands. Once back
at the cabin, Kyla realized how wet they'd become in
the stream. Luke had damp spots on his shirt and
wet patches on the seat of his jeans above where the
waders had ended.

"You can have the shower first," Luke said, stash-
ing his fishing gear out of the way in the side hall.

Kyla's mouth dropped open in disbelief. "Pardon?"

"Go ahead, you can shower before I do."

"Luke, you do have a cabin of your own to shower
in. And wouldn't you prefer fresh clothes afterward?"

"Barry and I are the same size. He leaves a wardrobe here. He won't mind if I borrow something for
the evening." He cocked his head to one side and
smiled at her with her arms crossing her chest in the
classical defensive position. "You aren't going to
make me walk clear around the lake, are you?"

"You'll have to eventually. Makes sense to do it
now in daylight so you can bring the jeep back when

you come for dinner. Otherwise, you'll find yourself walking back in the dark tonight."

"Maybe, maybe not. I'll shower first, then."

Apparently he considered his leaving tonight a debatable issue. He walked out of the kitchen, making himself thoroughly at home. He was taking a hell of a lot for granted, Kyla fumed. It was high time she took back control of her life and did the steering. She found the bathroom steaming up and Luke bare-chested. His shirt had been unceremoniously tossed to the blue-tiled counter. His fingers were at the waistband snap when Kyla flew into the tiny room. A huge grin accompanied the sound of the snap plucking free.

"Luke, that's enough . . ."

"I'll just keep on undressing, Kyla. You won't see anything you didn't get a good look at this morning."

She spun her back to him after he rolled down enough denim to expose his jutting hipbones and to remind her of his distaste for underwear. Damn the man! Sensing the futility of reasoning with him, Kyla groped for the doorknob and conceded bathroom privacy to Luke with a resounding slam.

How many women had he stripped for? Kyla wondered. Enough to be comfortably shameless with his own nudity! The probability that the number was enormous irritated her. That she was irritated increased her distress.

Dissecting the bloodless chicken on the kitchen cutting board proved therapeutically satisfying. Kyla believed in emotional control. Temper tantrums wasted valuable energy. Shouting matches ended with little more than sore throats. But there was something to be said for butchering a chicken.

Twenty minutes later Luke called out, "Your turn." Kyla wiped her hands on a dish towel, deciding to resolve the whole situation by rescinding the dinner invitation.

She walked into the bedroom with brisk determination, and came to a dead halt. Luke's rump was barely covered by a towel hardly bigger than a napkin. His arms were raised as he rubbed another towel over his wet hair. When he turned at her gasp, Kyla saw that the towel at his waist was embarrassingly inadequate, the knot riding low on his hipbone and the ends opened enough to expose the soft skin above his leg.

On the bed lay a creamy Irish knit sweater and burgundy cords. She stood dumbly, all her purposeful words dying in her throat as Luke said, "It's all yours." Her eyes slid up over his flesh to meet with his eyes. "The shower," he qualified with a grin.

"Didn't your mother ever teach you to wear clothes?" Kyla snapped. She turned on her heel and walked into the bathroom, closing the door.

Steam from Luke's shower still fogged the air of the little room, the mist heavy with the scent of Luke and soap and . . . intimacy, she thought. Barry's spare razor lay drying on the sink edge, but other than that, Luke had cleaned up after himself. Everything belonging to him was gone. Except the dark blue stain left by his wet feet on the pale blue rug, the round smear in the cloudy mirror he had dried off to watch himself shaving . . . and the scent. The overwhelming fragrance of him that made her head spin and shoved her heart down below her waist to beat with a slow, heavy pump.

Kyla moaned and turned away from her own besotted image in the mirror. She swayed dizzily and leaned on the cool tiles, pressing forehead and palms to the cold wall. *Pull yourself together, Kyla,* she ordered. What in the world was happening to her? She'd never been affected like this by *any* man, let alone a near-stranger.

She showered. She made the spray as icy as she could stand it, the bracingly cold water pulling her skin taut and shocking the passionate thoughts from her brain.

When she joined Luke in the living room her russet hair was slightly damp and shimmered against her green silk blouse. Like Luke, she was barefoot. The knife creases in her black slacks gave an illusion of length to her legs. Luke's gaze crept over her and she noted the lowering of his lashes, the nearly imperceptible press of his lips. Her heart seemed to tear loose, then skid to a halt. She curled her toes in the thick carpet, virtually digging her feet into the floor to keep from rushing to his arms.

Luke smiled. "I can't remember ever getting so much pleasure out of just looking."

He was different. Kyla sensed it. Not aloof or withdrawn exactly, but tentative, slowing down. Dinner conversation was labored, bumping along in fits and starts. Luke didn't seem to want small talk, and Kyla couldn't seem to begin a sentence that didn't fade off to nothing.

Together they cleared the dishes to the sink and left them for later. "Time for a fire," Luke said, going to the fireplace.

"Mmm. I guess. I almost hate to close the windows. You know what it smells like? Christmas. Like a fresh-cut pine tree sending its clean minty smell all over the house."

Luke chuckled. "You have a certain knack for finding something in the civilized world to explain life in the mountains."

I haven't found anything in the civilized world that explains you, she thought. She closed the last window and turned to see Luke throw his arms wide in a full body stretch. Thick clothing hid the ripple of muscle from Kyla's eyes, but her imagination saw each hard shimmer. Luke reached up with both hands and combed through his tumbled gold hair that had dried without benefit of brush. Loose, tired strides carried him to the sofa, where he dropped heavily into its inviting comfort. Seconds later he rearranged his weight, pulling his long legs up to sprawl the full length of the floral cushions. Kyla moved toward the sole chair and was stopped short of her destination by Luke catching her wrist. He tugged swiftly, unbalancing her. Only her rigid arms on the edge of the sofa saved her from winding up on top of him.

"No, Luke." She didn't trust herself to meet his eyes and so she dropped her gaze to his lean brown fingers braceleting her upper arms. She began to tremble, and this time the quaking had nothing to do with fear.

"What is it, Kyla? What?"

She shook her head, her hair falling over her shoulder. Luke brushed the rioting mass back, then let a finger trail slowly from her shoulder to her breast, circling the taut peak, before taking it back up to her face.

"Talk to me, Kyla." Luke tipped her chin up, forcing her eyes to meet his. "You know I want you. And I know you want me. But you keep pulling back. Why?"

"I just met you. I don't know you."

"It happens that way sometimes." He looked closely at her. "Is there any reason we shouldn't? I know you said you weren't married or involved. But . . . is there someone . . . we'd hurt?"

Yes, me. "It's not the right time, Luke. I've got other things going on and . . . and. . ."

"And what? You haven't got anything going on right now. We're the only ones here."

"And what better way to spend the time than bedroom acrobatics?" She jerked herself free and sat back on her heels. "I don't sleep around to while away idle hours."

"I didn't think you did."

"Didn't you? Oh, leave me alone, Luke." She pushed up from the floor and stood looking down at him. She spoke each word slowly and distinctly. "The fact remains—we just met yesterday."

"It doesn't feel like yesterday. It feels like I've known you, waited for you, for a long time."

That's what he had said—his first words to her—"I've been waiting for you." Kyla felt her resolve slip, and resisted the pull he had on her. He lay there waiting, and wanting her. She turned away. "It's time you put your own clothes on and went home. I have dishes to do." She fled to the kitchen and filled the sink with suds. She couldn't, she wouldn't. She had only to remember the disaster with Zach, whom she'd known and trusted, to reaffirm the painful knowledge that to give herself to someone was to give too much.

When Kyla returned to the living room, flames were lazily licking at the cherry wood, casting a dancing blush over the room. She cupped elbows in palms and went to the foot of the sofa, firm in her decision to evict Luke. His head was buried deep in the cushions and his eyes were closed.

"Luke," she whispered.

He didn't budge and she remembered how he had complained of not sleeping well the night before. Kyla's heart swelled with tenderness. "So, Mr. Mountain Man, you're not so tough after all."

She knelt at his side and gently nudged his shoulder. "Luke, wake up. You've got to go home."

He stirred slightly in his sleep. Kyla glanced at the blackened windows, remembering that he didn't have the jeep, and thinking of how cold and late it was. Could she drive him home? Of course not. And even if she were willing to take a chance with her car's delicate frame on that obstacle course, Luke wouldn't allow it. With a resigned sigh, she decided to leave him where he was.

She took a blanket from the linen closet and covered Luke, tucking the satin border of the blanket under his chin. She checked to make sure the screen was in place, sure he'd be warm enough by the fire. Then she turned out the last lamp and went to bed.

Four

Kyla woke slowly, pleasantly, floating from one impression to another, absorbing the new day with her senses.

The cabin's closed windows filtered the twitter of birds. Her quilted cocoon shed a delicious scent and she inhaled the heady drift. The same clean fragrance of Luke. He and Barry must use the same cologne, Kyla mused vaguely.

Then she was suddenly wide-awake. A pair of hands—large hands—had shoved her jersey night-shirt up to her neck while she'd slept. Wide palms were *glued* to her bare flesh. Long fingers were wrapped around her waist.

Kyla flew to a sitting position with a dawn-shattering scream.

Luke bolted up beside her, his eyes popping wide open. "My Lord, Kyla! Do you always wake up so . . . so suddenly?"

"You!" She grabbed the sheet that had fallen to her lap and drew it up to her chin. "You scared the . . . How . . . ?"

"Sh, sh," Luke pleaded. Pressing his fingertips to his temples, he grimaced. "Don't scream. Be as hysterical as you please . . . in a whisper." From beneath heavy lids, he considered her slightly flared nostrils, the rise and fall of her chest, her clenched fists. Mischief tugged at his mouth as he began reeling in the faded pink sheet. "What are you hiding, love? Hmm?"

The jersey had settled back around her with all the shield of a body stocking. Had it shrunk overnight? she wondered. Her breasts ached, swelled with the effort to contain the yearnings inflamed by the stroke of his languid gaze. Kyla tore her eyes from his rapt expression and glanced down, stunned at how deliberately the clinging knit detailed her aroused nipples. Fumbling uncertainly, she groped for the sheet and drew it back up to her chin, breathlessly demanding, "What were you doing to me?"

"I wasn't doing anything to you." Luke released a lungful of air in a long, drawn-out sigh and fell back to sprawl on the pillows piled at the headboard. "I was sleeping."

"Why?"

"Why wasn't I doing something to you? Or why was I sleeping?"

"Why were you sleeping *in my bed*?" A pulsing throb replaced the panic-stricken pace of her heart. Residual fear and kindling desire fused—one a clumsy tremble, the other subtler, a mere shiver. "Never mind why. Just get out!"

Luke drove his shoulders deeper into the pillows. Reaching out, he dragged his hand down the hair spilling past her shoulders. Selecting one willful curl, he wrapped it around his fist. "I don't wake up quite as abruptly as you, love. Lie in my arms and wake up slowly with me."

Hours of precisely that—lying in Luke's arms in any of a dozen intimate tangles—already had Kyla longing for the natural next step to union, clamoring for the touch that would release the tightly wound spring in her center.

She didn't lie down with him. She wasn't sure where she found the willpower to resist the gentle tugs he gave the strands of hair in his fist, but she was supremely grateful for it. He looked wonderfully rumpled from sleep, as perfectly disheveled as always. The collar of his turtleneck sweater had turned up, the creamy wool flirting with the soft underside of his unshaven jaw. His eyes, incredibly green by dawn's delicate light, watched her from beneath his mussed, sun-blessed hair as he carried one russet curl to his face, brushed its silky texture over one lean cheek, then touched it to his lips.

"Your hair smells of yesterday's wildflowers," he murmured.

"I doubt it," she said in a voice as low and unsteady. "I shampooed last night." He's beautiful but still masculine, Kyla thought. Soft voice and eyes, hard bone and muscle.

He dipped his face into the handful of dark hair and inhaled. "Wildflowers."

Suddenly Kyla resented every gorgeous inch of him. Resented every husky word of seduction he spoke, every fluid move toward her he took, every caress of his hands that obliterated rationality and turned her brain to mush.

She stiffened as the degree to which he'd manipulated her rose on her emotional barometer. The noticeable stiffening of her spine brought a quizzical hike to Luke's brow.

"Kyla?" He flinched at the cool stare she returned. "I have a reason for sleeping with you."

"Not one that'll be good enough for me."

Kyla threw off the sheet and started scrambling across the bed. Before she could swing her legs over the side, she'd been tackled and flipped onto her back, her arms pinned at either side of her head, the lower, naked half of her body trapped by Luke's rough corduroy-clad legs.

"I *do* have an explanation," he ground out through clenched teeth. "And you are going to listen to it."

"Because you aren't going to give me a choice." Kyla iced the words. Involuntary surrender. This was a position she had spent her life avoiding—rendered helpless to another's physical superiority, a victim of her own limits. As fear and desire continued to skirmish for petty control, raw, unbridled anger rushed up to dominate Kyla's emotions. Tears of humiliation threatened behind her eyes. Oh, no! she thought. Not tears! In the past two days she'd babbled like an idiot, blushed twice, and stamped her foot in a temper tantrum. If he made her cry, she'd *never* forgive him.

Kyla lashed out. "You're arrogant, a self-centered, thick-headed, stubborn, egotistical bully!"

"My! When you wake up, you *really* wake up."

Kyla glared back. "You'd better have one helluva reason."

"I was cold," Luke explained calmly. "You neglected to feed the fire before you went to bed, so it died out. I woke up around three or four in the morning, half-frozen. You were the closest source of heat to curl up next to and thaw out with."

"You were cold," Kyla drawled. "That's your excuse for everything. It's the same one you gave for humiliating me at the lake."

"Naked. This time I'm dressed."

"I know. Your belt buckle is drilling a hole in my stomach."

"You aren't listening." Luke redistributed his weight, relieving the least of her discomforts. "I'm dressed."

"Big deal!" Kyla snapped. "Most people over the age of two are, unless they're in a bathtub."

"I'm not most people." His dimpled grin both dazzled and infuriated Kyla . . . and he knew it. "If I'd planned to sample the sweet promise of your body in the middle of the night, love, you can bet I wouldn't have worn my pants to bed."

"You've been planning to make a full meal of me since I arrived in these mountains—with or without your pants on!" Kyla took control of the hysterical edge in her voice and finished in a tone that was calmer, cooler. "Now I'm going to explain something to you, you impossible bully. I'm tired of being the canary to your cat. Never has a woman been as persistently pursued by a man as I've been by you. I'll admit to being flattered—at first. Men don't look at me the way you do . . . they never have—"

"I don't believe that."

Kyla growled her frustration. What did it take to reach him? "Enough is enough! It's not flattering anymore. I've said no. I've asked you to leave me alone—"

"And we don't even have to touch. A look. A smile. That's all it takes. It's immediate . . . and it's mutual."

Kyla sighed wearily. "And it's physical." She was beginning to sound like a broken record. "It has no more substance or meaning than one of your mountain animals sniffing out another." Luke stiffened, the burden of his legs as painful as stone pillars on top of her. A cold mask slipped over his face. Well, he certainly didn't appreciate his amorous advances being compared to that of a none-too-particular amoral beast, she noted with satisfaction. Maybe she was finally getting it through his thick skull that that was how he made *her* feel. "I want more than that. I'm *worth* more than that."

Just then, when she thought she finally had her scuttled composure under control, her eyes pooled with tears to betray her. "Now get off me," she whispered as the first hot beads rolled into the hair at her temples.

Luke released her wrists, pushing up to kneel

between her legs. He held his arms up, palms out in an exaggerated hands-off gesture. Utterly drained, Kyla gazed up at him, feeling his anger wash down on her in one icy wave. *He* was angry? She rolled over and slid off the bed. She wanted to flee, to be blessedly alone and figure out what was happening to her. After conquering the urge to bolt twice, she was finally going to do it . . . too late to save herself. Snatching her robe from where it lay on the end of the bed, Kyla dashed into the bathroom and slammed the door.

She huddled, knees to chest, on the closed toilet seat. What an incredibly juvenile way to behave! she thought. And if she had to scamper off like a scared rabbit, she might have at least chosen the kitchen to run to. She could have paced in the kitchen . . . or calmed her ragged nerves with a five-course breakfast. Instead, she and her indignation were stuck in a claustrophobic room the approximate size of two shower stalls—half of which *was* a shower stall. Definitely not vice-presidential behavior!

The creaks and groans of the floor giving under Luke's bare feet leaked in from the generous crack under the door. Shadows of his pacing interrupted the splash of light there. She winced at the string of vicious expletives he hurled at the unimpressed slab of oak.

"Dammit, Kyla! You're overreacting. You know that, don't you?" His taps on the door were gentler than the exasperated demand, as were his next words. "You okay, love?" Silence. Two more taps. "Let me in, Kyla."

He was already "in" almost every place that mattered, Kyla admitted helplessly. He filled her thoughts and heart so fully she ached with it. Finding it impossible to be still, she wrapped and unwrapped her toes in the hem of her robe.

"Kyla?" Tap, tap, tap. "You're scaring me."

Good! He deserved it! A healthy dose of it! She smiled wryly, picturing Luke on the other side of the door, confused and frazzled. Uncertain what was taking place on the inside, or what he should do about it. And hating how inept the whole baffling mess made him feel. Kyla thought it just desserts that he taste the fare she'd been choking on the past few days.

"What are you doing, Kyla?"

I'm falling in love with you, you jerk. The thought, masquerading as a knot of despair in her stomach, unwound to seep into every fiber of her being. She loved him. Oh, Lord, never had she felt more like a babe in the woods. Her groan of despair was easily heard through the door.

"Dammit, Kyla!" Luke roared from the bedroom. "Open this door or I'll break it down!"

"It isn't locked," she called out. Kyla drew her knees tighter to her chest as Luke stepped into the tiny room. "There. See how simple things are when you behave like a *civilized* person?"

He plastered one open hand to the tile wall. The other curled into a bloodless fist that he leashed to his side by hooking his thumb on a belt loop. His brooding gaze silently considered her tiny, huddled form.

She was falling, all right, but she hadn't hit yet. Kyla searched within for the cool, efficient woman, trying to call on every experience from her past when she'd successfully bluffed a first-rate opponent while holding a fourth-rate hand. But all she found on the inside was a vulnerable heart too precariously close to being battered again. How? How had she let this happen?

The little room shrank around Luke's size and presence. What was he waiting for? she wondered. Gazing up, she returned his stare, no longer crying, but her wide, dark eyes still shimmered with her earlier tears.

"Damn those eyes," Luke muttered hoarsely. "Just like a marked doe looking down both barrels of a cocked rifle." He sighed and pushed one hand through his hair, leaving his fingers curled at the back of his neck. "I don't get it! We're so damn electric together we could light up the whole city of Los Angeles. We're both adults . . . no commitments to anyone else. We want each other! Yet every time I start making love to you, you wither like a terrified virgin at the hands of a rapist. I don't . . ."

The sentence faded away, unfinished. A husky sound rumbled deep in his chest. His groan of enlightenment filled the limited space between them. "Hasn't there been a man in your life, Kyla? Is that the problem?"

"Oh, Luke," Kyla moaned, dropping her forehead to her knees.

"I see," Luke mumbled.

He didn't see at all! Kyla's chest ached with a restrained scream. A terrified virgin? Terrified, yes. Her brief stab of initiation to womanhood didn't compare to the frightening experience filling Kyla's mind—of once clinging to a flying surfboard, suddenly a flimsy, careening life raft in the face of a powerful wave. All that turbulent force driving her at speeds too fast and lethal. That's what Luke was, Kyla thought. Another potent sample of Mother Nature's unleashed force—in the flesh—about to roll her over, drag her to helpless depths, then recede, leaving her on the brink of emotional death.

Without lifting her head, she mumbled into the fluffy material stretched over her knees, "There was a man once."

"What did you say, love?" Luke took a giant step and dropped to sit on his heels. Kyla pulled her head up, finding his soft, bright eyes only inches away. His breath played on her face, in warm plumes of moist air. His clean scent rippled through her.

"I said—yes, there was someone once." She closed her eyes slowly, then just as slowly opened them again. "And *that's* the problem."

A sharp flash of something shot through his features. Curious, Kyla thought, it almost resembled a wince of pain. Or maybe it wasn't that at all, but regret. He might have preferred her chaste . . . a tenderfoot in every sense.

"He hurt you."

Kyla nodded. "And I learned a valuable lesson from it: Sleeping with a man *isn't* part of getting to know him better. I don't trade names, shake hands, and pop into bed." She sighed and was quiet for a moment before continuing. "My mother used to say . . ." Kyla chuckled bitterly. Not in ridicule of her sweet, old-fashioned mother, with her rules and cautions and dire consequences, but at herself for having shrugged it off, dismissed all advice as the doomsday preaching of a neurotic. "She used to say my virginity was a treasure, a precious gift. And that somewhere in the big bad world, there waited a special man. Corny, huh?" Her head moved in a slow, negative shake. "It's true. It was precious. I had no idea how fragile a gift it was . . . until I gave it."

With the tip of a finger Luke traced the delicate bones of her hands so desperately clenched at her knees. Dark skin against ivory flesh. Fascinating how thoroughly opposite they were, she thought vaguely. Tall to short, big to small, brawn to brain, push to pull. She rested her cheek on her knee, closing her eyes to the appealing sight.

"He wasn't very special," she whispered huskily. "And he didn't consider anything I gave him fragile enough to merit much care . . . including my 'precious' passion."

A harsh expletive escaped from Luke's lips. Kyla was surprised and touched to see anguish in his taut features. "So he's the one that made my beautiful doe gun-shy."

"We were engaged to be married. I loved him. It should have been perfect with him." Her lips twisted in poor imitation of a smile and her voice grew bitter. "But then, I never was a very *physical* person."

There were no words—nor was Kyla inclined—to describe aptly the devastation, the knowledge that her body had once again proved inadequate. She was a woman with a keenly developed mind trapped in a body that consistently failed her.

"I made such an awful mistake with Zach. I don't ever again want to hurt that much and survive."

"Zach." Luke spat the name as he might a foul taste in his mouth.

"Zachary Fullerton."

"I didn't want to know his name," Luke muttered.

"You didn't want!" Kyla cried. "That's all I've heard for two days—what you do and don't want. Now it's my turn. And what *I* want is for you to leave me alone."

"I'd never hurt you, Kyla. You must know that."

"Yes, you will," Kyla countered with surprising sureness in her soft voice. "You'll hurt me. You may not mean to. I know you don't *want* to. But I'll come away from an affair with you hurting like hell." Kyla looked him straight in the eye. "Go away, Luke."

He touched the pouty fullness of her bottom lip. Kyla drew back to sever the tenuous connection, and Luke stood up. His hand dived into her sleep-tousled hair to comb the wild strands. Sifted by his fingers, the ends floated in a fiery mantle around her face. Kyla realized he was leaving, knew he had finally *heard* her, prayed she wouldn't prevent his going. She bit her lips to prevent the rush of words that would stop him—and bring her exquisite pleasure, unbearable pain.

He closed the door of the little room behind him.

He didn't kiss me today, Kyla thought sadly, and rammed her knuckles to her mouth.

She jumped up and twirled the shower taps until hot water thundered from the shower head. She didn't want to hear him in the bedroom exchanging Barry's clothes for his own. Didn't want to hear any of the sounds punctuating his departure—no bureau drawers opening, no chink of trouser-pocket change, no bedroom door closing.

When Kyla stepped out of the steamy bathroom, once again wrapped in her thick robe, she stared at the rumpled sheets on the bed, feeling colder than she had her first night in the cabin without heat. She couldn't conjure up one memory of having slept in Luke's arms. She wished she could.

Beth Gainer glanced away from the large picture window she had been gazing out of when her husband ushered Kyla into the bedroom. Preoccupied with Luke, but with enough presence of mind to remember her friendly overture of the day before, Kyla had mechanically simmered the ingredients for chicken soup that morning. Sealing the hearty broth in an airtight container, she'd walked the lake path to the cabin behind Pop's store. Despite its cottagelike exterior, the house Kyla had just passed through to reach the bedroom was furnished with durable permanence. This was a home, she thought, not a seasonal retreat, made special by Jake and Beth Gainer, two people she had begun to care for because Luke did.

Pearly sunlight, astir with dust motes, streamed over the frail, doll-like woman resting in a spindleback rocking chair. A scarlet afghan covered her knees and trailed from her lap to pour a vermilion pool on the gleaming wood floor.

"Beth? This is Luke's girl, Kyla," Jake said by way of introduction. Kyla's breath caught in her throat at the possessive implication. "She's brought some chicken soup. Homemade."

"My dear child, how thoughtful of you. Please come in and sit with me." Beth gracefully swept the air with her slim arm, indicating a plump, flowered easy chair, as Jake relieved Kyla of the soup container. "Well, come on, I'm not contagious, if that worries you."

Kyla laughed as she entered the room. "I'm not worried. And I'm not Luke's—"

"You just missed him. He left not ten minutes ago."

Kyla sank to the chair conveniently angled to face Beth, wondering if the distinct warmth trapped in the cushion might be Luke's lingering body heat. Without letting her smile slip, she said quite firmly, "I'm not Luke's girl."

Periwinkle-blue eyes smiled back at her. "You're a liberationist?"

"A what?"

"One of those women's-libbers who won't be called girl? Or toots, baby, sweetie . . ." The blue eyes virtually danced as Beth ticked the pet names off. Kyla chuckled even as she recalled a baritone voice murmuring "love" and "tenderfoot." Beth's voice dropped to a conspiratorial whisper. "I'm a discredit to my sex, I'm afraid. I've always secretly enjoyed an occasional wolf whistle."

Kyla laughed out loud. "Well, that's not what I meant. I'm not Luke's *anything*."

"Oh, I understand." Not even Beth's gentle smile creased her unwrinkled skin. Her flawless complexion resembled parchment smoothly paving the fragile bones of her face and hands, the only flesh exposed by the high neck and long sleeves of her flannel nightgown. "No one belongs to anyone these days. Free and easy. Right?"

Kyla swiftly rejected further attempts to correct the woman's misconception, preferring to drop the subject of Luke Hudson altogether. "So how are you feeling today, Mrs. Gainer?"

"Beth, please. And I feel as fit as a dishrag. Restored to health, but still weak and sloppy. When you're seventy-two you spend more time recovering than you do being ill." She sighed tiredly and let her head droop to one side.

"I shouldn't stay, then."

"Please don't go. At least sit with me while Jake heats the soup."

"If you're sure I won't tire you." Kyla glanced around the comfortable room at the four-poster bed, each post as thick as a tree trunk; at the incredibly high mattress and the quaint set of steps at the bed-side; at *his* reading glasses resting on an open book on one night table and *her* wicker sewing basket wait-ing on the other.

When Kyla brought her eyes back to Beth she had the distinct feeling that she too had been given a thor-ough examination.

"Yes. You are every bit as lovely as Luke said you were."

Solemn vows to banish the man from her mind disintegrated. "He talked about me?"

"At great length." Wispy eyebrows lifted, asking how Kyla could doubt it. "The eyes—he's quite taken with them. Big brown eyes, he said, that make a man wish he were in her arms—and if not, then in another state."

Something bumped into Kyla's stomach, proba-bly her gullible heart. Had that big, arrogant man really sat in this room confiding such precious thoughts to this frail old woman?

"Which is probably why he's on his way to Phoenix, Arizona."

"Phoenix? Luke's left the mountains?" Kyla cried.

"There, you see. You *are* his girl." Beth began rocking her chair with tiny taps of her feet to the floor.

It's just as well, Kyla decided, consciously smoothing the lines of distress from her forehead. It wasn't quite what she'd had in mind when she'd asked him to leave—a hike to his side of the lake would have been adequate. Well, the news guaranteed he wouldn't be sitting on her doorstep when she returned. So why didn't relief ease the cold bands lacing her chest?

As if sensing her ambiguous feelings and knowing the words to ease them, Beth announced, "He'll be back, though. He doesn't let go that easily. There is no middle ground with Luke."

"I've noticed," Kyla said, smiling despite herself.

"He shuns or shadows. So intense. Even as a boy." Beth gazed out the window, her profiled brow furrowed with intent as her memory peopled the uninhabited view. "How he adored his father. Copied his walk and stance. Mimicked his voice and laugh. Wherever Mike Hudson was, that's where you'd find Luke. Except Mike's workshop. No one went in there. Then Luke would go off to . . . wherever it was he went . . . alone."

The stream, Kyla thought. To his rock that fit him so well.

"Those were the years." Beth sighed. Bewildered sadness filled her damp blue eyes. "Few of them come anymore. Except Luke. He seems to have a need that is only satisfied here . . . the way others go home. Strange, though. The Hudsons bought their cabin when Luke was about eight years old. It was never more than a summer home. Yet, it's as if Luke were born here."

Beth's words bruised the walls of Kyla's heart. She envisioned a small boy nursing a pain so private he shunned outsiders, so deep he shadowed those he loved. *Oh, don't, Kyla,* she ordered herself. *Isn't the man hard enough to reject? Don't complicate things by adding a dejected little boy to the picture.*

"Soup's on," Jake called out.

Kyla stood and helped Beth to her feet. "Don't you fret, dear." Beth patted Kyla's cheek. "He'll be back, I'm sure of it."

* * *

If the vice-presidency of CompuMart were dangled as enticement, Kyla still couldn't have said whether the anxiety building within her was because Luke *would* return, or, dear Lord, because he might not. She lounged on the dilapidated dock, her back resting against the least feeble of the six support piles. It was early morning and she basked in the first beams of sunlight, wearing a daringly styled white maillot bathing suit. She'd spent too many months in an office to risk exposing her pale complexion to the sharper afternoon rays.

No matter how many times she turned her thoughts elsewhere, they persisted in backtracking to the morning Luke, so magnificently naked, had stood in this very same spot. With a troubled sigh she tried to recall how she'd originally planned to fill the time during her week in the mountains. In the two days since Luke's departure, Kyla had put up with all the peace and quiet, rest and relaxation she cared to suffer. Morning walks, cooking for one, and dropping in on Beth barely took her to lunchtime.

A rummaging through her car's glove compartment the day before had produced a back issue of *Personal Computer*. She'd begun flipping through it, but the exhilaration had been short-lived. Before long she began wondering what Brad and Chuck were up to, whether Andrew Carson had made his decision yet.

She told herself she spent the better part of her time on the dock because the rooms of the cabin were haunted by Luke Hudson. Every inch of space evoked his spirit—filling the generous furniture, shoulder-to-jamb in the doorways, laughing in the perpetual silence. Of course the excuse didn't hold water—of all Kyla's memories, the one of Luke on this dock was the most riveting.

Luke.

She hadn't expected to fall in love this way. Suddenly, unexpectedly . . . frantically. That's what disturbed her the most. The racing pulse, the shortness of breath, the inability to think when he was near. She'd never reacted to a man this way before. If this was love, then she hadn't loved Zach.

With him, things had moved slowly, unerringly, and quite naturally along a logical path to a destination that had seemed inevitable. He and Kyla had shared a career, met as colleagues, and moved on to friendship. Gradually they'd drawn closer, until the blending just came to be. Her blood hadn't boiled like molten lava. The world hadn't spun out of control. Her failure to scream and scratch in the throes of ecstasy, Zach had described as "dysfunction." So Kyla never admitted she hadn't felt fulfilled. She'd craved warmth and a sense of belonging from the relationship, and that was exactly what she'd gotten.

Besides, she seriously doubted that all this misery, no matter how exquisite, had anything to do with the type of love that endured, that lasted a lifetime. She couldn't imagine going through life gasping for breath while her heart was running a forty-yard dash. It was downright unhealthy.

Grabbing the plastic bottle of sunscreen, Kyla filled her cupped palm and covered her arms, luxuriating in the cool bath of cream. More than likely, she decided, these were the symptoms of lust. And once the curiosity was satisfied and the itch scratched—then what?

Refilling her palm with cream, she began a cool massage of her legs. But what if it were love? she wondered. She had given her heart once and been terribly hurt. It was understandable that she would be more cautious the next time. But five years? Had she really lived five years alone and unloved? Not alone, she reminded herself. She'd dated plenty of wonderful men, more than she could count, or even remember. Neighbors, friends of friends, all forgettable. She didn't want to spend her life nursing a wound to the extent it became her obsession. Zach had robbed two years of her life. If she allowed him to steal her future, it would be her own damn fault.

"Turn around, love, I'm behind you." Luke's soft voice washed over her. He stood in a shaft of sunlight at the juncture of dock and land wearing much-abused tennis shoes and white shorts. And the sight of him quickened everything inside of her. Would this always happen to her? *Lord, he was so beautiful*, she thought.

Her hands skimmed the ankle of one leg, and she slowly completed the stroke, wanting to pull his languorous gaze along the path her hands took. Luke complied, following her graceful moves over gently curved calf and firmly toned thigh. Her heart stopped, then galloped ahead. Downright unhealthy? Could be fatal, in fact, she decided.

Striding over the boards, he stopped inches from Kyla's legs, dropping to sit on his heels. His hand wrapped the curve of her arch, his eyes fixed on her mouth.

"I thought you were in Arizona," Kyla muttered stupidly, stalling the lips that were about to bestow the kiss she was dying to receive.

"Mm-hmm." Then his lips claimed hers. The kiss was warm and welcoming, a reacquaintance of lips, an embrace of tongues. It seemed the most natural way to greet him. He lifted her hand from where it lay curved at her thigh, pulling her to her feet. "Let's go to your cabin. I have a proposition for you."

"You always have a proposition for me."

Kyla caught the laugh twinkling in his eyes. "Not like this one, love. You may have to sit down for this one."

"Oh, really? We haven't gotten to the basics and you're getting kinky?"

His clasp on her hand was loose, a mere mingling of fingers. His thumb drew soft circles on her palm, creating lovely flutters in her breast. Luke pulled her to the path and stopped abruptly, pointing at Kyla's small pink-painted toes. "Shoes."

"No, feet," Kyla quipped.

"Put your shoes on, Kyla."

"I didn't wear any."

His eyebrows shot up. "You mean you walked barefoot from your cabin? How *uncivilized*," he reprimanded her with mock primness. He turned to the path. "Ever felt a snake under your foot?"

"Snake?" Revulsion shuddered through her.

Then she was swept up in his arms. "Tenderfoot, how in the world did you manage to stay in one piece for two whole days without me?"

Kyla rested her head on his shoulder, a small smile on her lips. Barely, she thought. One breath at a time.

Five

"*Hike the mountains!*" Kyla repeated Luke's proposal as he set her down in the kitchen—adding several decibels to his "oh, by the way" delivery. "That's a *crazy* proposition! Why not 'Come see my etchings,' or 'How about a quickie'? I've rehearsed the answers to those."

"I don't etch and I'm never quick."

He had carried her all the way to the cabin, rattling nonstop on a subject that so fascinated him he'd showered her with a baritone explosion of words. Rather than listen to the content, Kyla had melted into her cradle of supple muscle and luxuriated in the deep velvet voice. Now she recalled phrases like "the injustice of stamping out someone's spirit" and "a moral obligation to encourage courage."

"Put 'er down, Kyla." He dropped his gaze to her clenched fists. "You look a bit unsteady."

Eyeing him warily, she slumped into the rattan seat of the nearest chair. Maybe it was the sort of idea that grew on one, she thought. "Climb a mountain," she ventured aloud. No. It wouldn't even take root.

"I'd inadvertently kill myself. If I'm a lousy fishing companion, I'd be a lethal hiking partner."

"Oh, you were lousy at fishing, all right."

Behind the drawled sarcasm lay a compliment that coaxed a lopsided grin from Kyla. "Come to think of it, I *was* pretty good . . . for a beginner. But mountains? I'm so inexperienced—"

"I'm not."

"I don't know a hiking trail from a dry riverbed."

"I do."

"I'm not very strong—"

"You've only got to carry yourself."

Patience deserted her. Damn the man! He still couldn't take no for an answer! Kyla unequivocally accepted her shortcomings as well as her strengths. She resisted expounding on either. "You aren't suggesting a simple sightseeing tour, but a dangerous—and potentially disastrous—undertaking."

"You'd be safe with me, love."

He let the huskily uttered promise hang in the space between them while he lit a cigarette. Confronting even more persuasion in his eyes, Kyla dropped her gaze, focusing on the cupped hand from which smoke curled lazily. She noticed the sensitive fingers, the graceful composition of bone. She knew and remembered the exquisite skill of that hand to touch, to tease. Competent hands that nurtured and protected, built fires, fixed generators, netted game, and returned it to nature. Yes, she'd be safe in those hands. . . .

Lord! She was actually considering it! Pitting her ninety-six pounds against eight thousand feet of forest and rock! "Breakfast! How does a bacon-lettuce-and-tomato sandwich sound to you?" Leaping to her feet, she ran to the cupboard, pulling out a loaf of bread. Luke flicked his cigarette into the sink before lifting the spongy package from her hands and returning it to the shelf with an overhand toss.

"How the hell can you be so tiny? You want to eat

all the time." The fingers of both hands coasted up her bare arms, the fleeting touch shivering over her skin. Other flesh, that bared by the adventurous cut of her bathing suit, thrilled to the stroke of his eyes. Slipping his thumbs under her shoulder straps, he used the thin bands to draw her closer to his bare legs and chest.

"I eat when I'm nervous."

"And you're nervous now?"

Actually, she thought, the tender clamp of his arms, the pulse of his heartbeat under her palm, was giving birth to something else entirely. "Talking about death-defying feats tends to plant lilies in my liver."

"Take the chance, Kyla."

"But why?" It was an earnest, urgent question.

"Because, city girl, you're only half-alive. You sit on the sidelines playing intellectual games and call it living. You've gone so far beyond cautious, you're numb. In more ways than one." That hurt. She responded to the verbal slap with a sharp gasp. "No, love, don't pull away from me. You're missing so much, Kyla. With a little guidance, some confidence, you can do it. I know you can."

Resistance seeped out of her like sand sucked away by the ocean tide. After a lifetime of wet blankets telling her "don't" and "can't," there stood her own private cheerleader urging her to go for it—and she wasn't quite sure what to do with him.

"Come with me." His voice was plaintive. She heard hope in the simple words, fervent and strangely fragile. This is special, the warmth of his eyes said. This is for you. "I'll give you the sun on fire in a sky of purple satin, the dawn spilling pink light into a sleepy valley. I'll give you the fragrance of pine and earth and mountain flowers, a symphony of wild birds. I'll show you how to *feel* life, and believe in yourself. Come see my world, love. Go to the top with me."

Fear knotted her stomach. Cold terror. But of what? Kyla wondered. Of daring to try? Or of knowing how precious the gift he offered was and not embracing it wholeheartedly? "How . . . how long does it take to get to the top of a mountain?"

He flashed that extraordinary thousand-watt smile. "You've already driven most of the way."

Squirming loose of his arms, she narrowed her brown eyes suspiciously. "How long?"

From the kitchen window they could see the mountaintop—a jagged pinnacle of rock penetrating shadowy treetops—and Luke inclined his head in thoughtful deliberation. "At a tenderfoot's pace? Three days—two to go up and one to come down."

And two nights together, she thought. More than unhealthy, loving him could be just plain dangerous. "When do we leave?"

Kyla put one foot forward and the rest was inevitable. She careened around the kitchen like a runaway football, propelled by the weight of the backpack strapped to her shoulders. She tripped into the cabinets, bounced off and hit the cool surface of the refrigerator, spun one and a half rotations and was heading for the door when Luke, laughing, grabbed her bouncing braid as she stumbled by him and reined her in.

They were at his cabin, where the closets had been ransacked for two of everything: backpacks, waterproof tarps, sleeping bags, canteens, compasses. While Kyla had locked up her own cabin, Luke had selected her wardrobe—every stitch sturdy, durable, and horribly unfeminine. Her first words upon entering the Hudsons' place had been, "Chintz? Chintz and ruffles? Not your style, Luke."

"Not my cabin. Here, try these boots on. They belong to my mother."

"You don't approve of my basic blacks?" Kyla had

asked, tightening the rawhide laces. Luke delivered a murderous glare at the high-heeled boots she'd kicked off. His fifth at least—as if the cow that made them wasn't already dead. "Perfect fit! And to think the same woman who puts chintz and ruffles on her furniture leaves lumberjack boots in her closet."

Three days' worth of nonperishable food, their clothes, and half a hardware store had been stowed in the backpacks. To the top of each bulging canvas sack he'd secured an insulation-lined bedroll. Luke had gently eased one of the contraptions onto Kyla's back and then she'd zipped around the room like a deflating balloon. As a test run, it was a total washout.

"You said I only had to carry myself."

"I lied."

"No kidding. You do know a hiking trail from a dry riverbed, don't you? You didn't lie about that too?"

"Generally, men carry packs weighing forty pounds, women thirty. I've lightened yours to twenty-five. You'll manage it."

"Wait a minute! If I'm supposed to have thirty pounds, I want thirty pounds. I won't have you carrying my load."

Amazement—or amusement—lifted his eyebrows. "Less than an hour ago you considered this trip with all the enthusiasm of a walk to the hanging tree. Now you want to carry the rope and tie the noose!"

"I want to hike the mountain, not be carried up. You'll guide me, but I'm going to do it. I want to work just as hard, to go just as high as you. Understand?"

"Mm-hmm. You want pain, sweat, and satisfaction. You'll get plenty carrying twenty-five pounds. Survival rule number one: Take no *less* than you need and no *more* than you can carry. You've got all the essentials—"

"Hah! You say that after taking away my makeup?"

"You're going *with* twenty-five pounds, Kyla, and *without* makeup."

Capitulation was immediate. She'd made her point. Whenever possible, Kyla meant to draw on her own resources, such as they were. Truth to tell, five more pounds and she'd have to crawl up on her knees.

"Steady on your feet?" His hands on her shoulders anchored her in place. "Before you try again, find your center of gravity."

"Look over there by the refrigerator. That was one helluva crash, it probably fell off."

With one hand he pressed her stomach toward her backbone while the other eased her chest forward. She felt like an upright drunk, standing at an angle that put her chin past her toes. With his index finger he drew an imaginary line from the back of her shoulders to the front of her thighs. "Keep that line vertical to the ground. Got it?"

"Got it."

"Good. Try moving it." He stepped back—to the very perimeter of the room, Kyla noticed.

"Oh, ye of little faith," she said sanctimoniously, and snorted, then took an experimental walk. "Eureka! It works on linoleum! 'Course I can't promise what'll happen on boulders."

"Faith? You call that faith?" At the stubborn lift of her chin Luke buried his laughter behind the checklist. "Let's finish outfitting you."

"Finish! What more? Long-sleeved shirt, heavy-duty jeans, two pairs of socks—one thin, one thick, as instructed—twenty-pound boots, bed and board on my back, and musk oil for perfume. I'm a cinch for a *Field and Stream* centerfold. By the way, you were going to explain the socks."

His knuckles skimmed her stomach as he unbuckled her belt, stirring up more butterflies to add to those already fluttering madly. Kyla didn't bother to ask why he now wanted to strip her. The moment she'd put her life in his hands, everything else had hopped in as well—her better judgment, her resistance . . .

"Doubling your socks prevents blister-causing friction."

He removed only her belt, running the slotted end through the carry-ring of a flashlight, then rethreading the leather strap so the flashlight hung at her right hipbone. His gaze never strayed from her face as his arms went around her waist, fingers blindly searching each loop. Special attention was given her tongue as she dragged its moisture along her dry lower lip. She wasn't nearly as numb as he thought, she decided.

He reached for one more item to hang on her left side.

"What's that?" she asked, as if it weren't obvious. The leather sheath covering the hatchet's blade failed to gild the menacing tool.

"What does it look like?"

"Excess baggage. I won't use it, Luke."

"You'll use whatever you have to"—he tugged the belt through the buckle, hauling Kyla next to his body—"*if* you have to. Your life may depend on it."

How absurd! she thought. In the middle of a kitchen, midmorning, equipped to withstand the worst in any of the four seasons, sexual tension began crackling in the air around them. Luke lifted her hands from his shirtfront and placed them on each side of his face. At the first light contact of her fingertips on his flesh, his eyes closed briefly. Not even Luke's long arms fit around Kyla *and* the stuffed pack. Sliding his hands down her sides, his palms lingered at the swell of her breasts, his thumbs dragging, pulling her cotton shirt taut.

Feathering her lips with a kiss, he watched her

eyes. When the russet-flecked brown glazed to soft liquid sable, he took her mouth fully.

Fingers spread on his rugged cheeks, Kyla felt his kiss with her hands. When his mouth opened to taste her, her palms received the ridge of his hard jaw. When he nuzzled the satin flesh inside her lower lip, her thumbs moved with the suckling hollows beneath his cheekbones.

She filled him with a sigh, he filled her with a deep-throated groan. Cupping her bottom, he lifted her up and against him. Abruptly the sweet plundering ended. Pain forced her eyes open as each cheek of her buttocks was clenched in the powerful grip of Luke's hands.

"Now, *what* have I found here?" The snug fit of her jeans was no deterrent to his deft fingers. Slipping them into her back pockets, he drew out two cylinders.

Adopting an innocent expression, Kyla studied the contraband. "Uh, that"—she pointed to the fat, long tube of mascara—"is Midnight Eyes. And that"—a nod at the shorter lipstick—"is Passion Fruit." Plucking them from his fingers, she returned them to her pockets. "And they *are* going with me. They fit the criteria—I *do* need them, I *can* carry them."

Green eyes danced with the humor he bit his lip to suppress. "Midnight Eyes and Passion Fruit, hmm?" And then his full-bodied laughter filled the room, poured warmly down her spine. Taking her hand, Luke pulled her across the kitchen and out the door.

With a wistful glance of farewell, Kyla turned her back on the community of cottages and followed Luke into the dense pine forest. She was incredibly proud of herself for agreeing to this. She was also scared to death.

An easy hike brought them to his fishing rock.

"We'll walk the bank most of today," Luke explained. "Got the feel of that pack yet?"

"Mmm. Much as I try to ignore it," Kyla said dryly.

With the toe of his boot he rolled a fallen limb over, then picked it up and nodded approval of the waist-high specimen. "It helps going uphill." He waited and Kyla realized she was supposed to find one for herself.

Looking around, she spotted one that seemed the right length. Bending from the waist, she reached out, then suddenly found her head rushing between her legs. Her feet left the ground and the world turned upside down as the weight of the pack flipped her onto her back.

When she opened her eyes, Luke was bent over her, his features tight with anxiety. "Kyla? Love?"

"Tell me, Luke. Was it a nice somersault? Did I have good form?"

He sat back on his heels, sighing with relief. "So-so. A little more practice and you'll have it down pat. Next time you want to pick something up, bend from your knees, stoop down. Keep your head higher than the pack."

With absolute confidence she waved away his offer of a hand up. "No, I got myself down here, I'll get myself up." Easier said than done, she discovered. Clumsily fighting her way onto her stomach, she tried a frontal approach. The minute her hands left the ground, her chest met it.

"Sure I can't help?" Luke asked.

She lay helpless as a turtle on her back.

"You're making it much harder than it is, love."

She perfected her somersault.

"A thousand and one ways *not* to get up."

Finally, crawling on all fours, she made it to a tree and pulled herself up its trunk.

"Stubborn," Luke muttered with a shake of his head.

"Standing!" Kyla announced, flashing a victor's

smile. Bending at the knees, she picked up her walking stick. "Ready?"

By the time they had hiked along the bank an hour, Kyla's enthusiasm had declined in direct proportion to the mountain's incline. No wonder the current in the stream was so swift. The pitch was deceptively steep—hardly noticeable until one walked against it. If it hadn't been for the occasional level ground, Kyla would have been defeated at the outset.

When a high-noon sun glared overhead and the land was flat enough for the stream to collect in a quiet, rippling pool, Luke suggested they stop and have lunch.

"Put 'er down, Kyla," he said, shrugging the pack from his back.

" 'Er may never get up again," Kyla warned, falling to a boulder, only to bounce to her feet with a yelp. Both hands flew to her back pockets and the forgotten makeup tubes. Luke suppressed a deserved "I told you so," but the sardonic lift of one eyebrow adequately communicated the sentiment. Kyla pitched the frivolous makeup into the pond. "Excess baggage," she muttered.

Lunch was simple, cold, and adequate. Replete and relishing sips of icy water dipped from the pool, Kyla alternated handfuls of crunchy nuts with juicy orange segments. And studied Luke. Resting in the shade of a lofty pine, his back to the slick trunk, he propped his elbows on raised knees, letting his hands hang between his legs. His jeans were old, worn white in places. He'd rolled up the sleeves of his deep red shirt to expose sinewy forearms, and pulled the snap front open to just above his belt buckle. Shaggy blond hair fringed his chest.

With no discernible movement, he launched a nut with the flick of his thumb. Then another. Something in the brush had captured his attention. And then Kyla saw the chipmunk poke its nose out from under a thorny bush. Luke made a purring sound in his throat and flipped another nut, this one landing close enough to the timid ball of fur to entice it from its haven.

So soft, the expressions of that rugged face, she thought. So graceful, the big, long body. She already knew the fierce turbulence of being wanted by this man, and wondered at the heart-squeezing miracle of being loved by him.

A shadow moved over Kyla, drawing her eyes up to the skies. "Uh . . . Luke?" Her voice quavered, her eyes locked on the predator gliding overhead. "Why is that vulture circling?"

A dimpled grin drove creases down his cheeks. "That's an eagle, tenderfoot. A bald eagle."

"Really! Our national bird?" Kyla jumped to her feet, face lifted to the sky, grinning at the magnificent creature. "Look at his wingspan! Isn't he the grandest thing you've ever seen? An American bald eagle. In person!"

She watched the eagle glide effortlessly on wind currents until he was swallowed by the horizon. With a sigh of contentment she pulled her gaze from the empty blue above to have it meet with the pleasure-filled light in Luke's eyes.

"I'm glad you like him, love," he said softly.

Feeling foolish suddenly, Kyla sat down again. Imagine, making such a big deal over a bird! "I've seen them in zoos . . ." she mumbled sheepishly. "But it's not the same."

"No, it's not the same. Clip the wings of an eagle, you might as well cut out his soul."

He's talking about himself, Kyla realized. A man who returned to the mountains the way others went home probably hated the confinement of the city. An unmarried, unemployed man who thumbed his nose at underwear undoubtedly hated confinement of any sort.

He took a thirsty pull on his canteen, then

poured what was left over his head. Kyla did the same, drenching herself with the heavenly cold water.

Opening waterlogged lashes, she saw Luke shaking his head, grimacing as if she had done something especially stupid. "Your shirt is soaking wet," he admonished her.

Of course her shirt was wet! She glanced at his broad, dry shoulders. Come to think of it, he *had* bent forward, wetting only his hair and face. "What dire thing will happen to me?" Kyla asked huffily.

"Blisters where your backpack rubs."

"Blisters."

"Get the spare shirt from your pack, tenderfoot. I'll fill our canteens and clean up camp while you change."

About to duck into the thick pines with her dry shirt, Kyla hesitated. "Uh . . . is there anything I should watch out for?"

Luke was crouched at the water's edge and didn't bother to look up. "You'll be fine. If anything comes up and you need me, just whistle." He glanced over his shoulder at her. "All kidding aside, you *do* know how to whistle, don't you?"

She couldn't resist! "Sure. Just put your lips together . . ." She leaned closer. "Curl your tongue, insert two fingers, and . . ." Her shrill whistle blew him right on his backside. "That's one thing my brothers *did* teach me. For the times I braved the world without one of them as a bodyguard. One whistle and they were there in a flash."

His rumbling laughter followed her into the woods. After changing her shirt, she took care of other personal matters in the privacy of the foliage. That was particularly awkward. "Oh, hell," she muttered, "and I thought the cabin lacked luxuries!"

Surprisingly, Kyla found she was anxious to get going. They kept to the stream's divergent course and conversation rose or dwindled depending on Kyla's ability on the steeper inclines. The atmosphere became rarefied, thin and harder to breathe. She stopped, slumping against a tree, greedily sucking up the oxygen-reduced air. Luke frowned when he saw the hand she raised to her chest, her fingers clawing her blouse material.

He came to her, gently sponging the film of perspiration from her face and neck. "We'll rest awhile."

"Just till I acclimate."

"It takes thirty days at this altitude."

"Never mind. I didn't pack enough clothes." Kyla smiled weakly. "Could we slow down?"

Settling fingers in the hollow of her throat, he tracked her laboring pulse. His thumb skimmed her lips. He smiled softly, his gaze showering her with admiration. "You're something else, love. One helluva fighter."

That atmosphere, so thin and deficient moments ago, grew tangible with the scent of Luke. As if he had evaporated and she was able to inhale him. His eyes lingered on her lips, parted by her soft pants. Kyla heard the breeze sough in the trees. His breath warmed her cheek as he angled his head, and she heard the throaty rasp of it, coming ever closer. His lips hovered above her mouth as gold-tipped lashes veiled his eyes, and she heard . . . "Thunder!"

Luke blinked. "What?"

"I hear thunder. Oh, Luke, it can't. What'll we do up here if it storms?"

He pressed his forehead to hers. "Thunder," he repeated. "Woodpeckers, radio static, now thunder."

Cradling her face in both hands, he smiled down at her with deep green eyes. "Come with me, tenderfoot. I'll show you thunder . . . the mountain's thunder."

He veered from the trail, moving slowly, parting tangled branches and checking on her progress every few paces. Instead of rolling across the sky to an angry crescendo before fading away, the grumbling built in intensity. At the base of a rock pile Luke slid free of his pack, then helped Kyla remove hers.

"Watch where I step and aim for the same spot. Test your foothold before putting your weight down."

Kyla visualized an avalanche depositing her, Luke, and half the mountain in the middle of downtown Los Angeles, and began backing away. "On second thought, why don't you just tell me what's on the other side?"

"You've come to see and feel, Kyla. You shouldn't see eagles in the zoo."

She studied the placing of his thick-soled boots with the intensity of following him through a landmine field. Even though she tested each hold, her heart lurched with the shift of her weight. Luke reached the top and leaned down to help her to the summit.

Kyla considered the hand he offered and rejected it. "I think I can make it."

He stepped back and watched her do just that. From the top she gazed back at the boulders she'd just climbed. Was she crazy? Risking such a daring and foolish stunt in order to be the subject of Luke's admiration? She'd have to watch that, she decided.

Without saying a word, Luke turned her in the circle of his arms, hugging her back to his chest. Before them lay a tucked-away Garden of Eden. "There. The mountain's thunder."

A sheet of turbulent wet silver poured from the lip of a towering rock wall, cascading to a lake foaming with the force of the waterfall. "Oh, Luke, it's gorgeous . . . beautiful. Can we stay awhile?"

"Can't waste daylight, love." She rolled her head on his chest and looked up at him, the disappointment evident in her gaze. "Damn those eyes," he groaned. "All right. Ten minutes. Hop down."

Wildflowers abounded. The greenery was rich, nurtured to lush vibrancy by the vapor rising from the foaming pool. Kyla's face grew shiny with the floating moisture. Her eyes sparkled with the wonder that surrounded her. "A miracle," she murmured.

Luke tipped her dew-kissed face up with a gentle finger. "Mm-hmm. A little bit of wild beauty beating the odds. I'm glad you like my world."

"I love your world." It was the closest she'd come to saying "I love you." Kyla wanted to gather every riotous pleasure the wild land and this wonderful man offered. Rising to her toes, she softly touched her misted lips to his mouth.

As she fell back onto her heels, Luke's mouth followed her down, kissing her deeply and fully. Kyla's insides churned as violently as the lake receiving the waterfall's onslaught. A promise of bliss filled each brush of his mouth on her eyelids, her throat, her lips again.

"Kyla . . . love . . ."

"Mmm . . ." Her breath came rapid and fast. Luke dropped his hand to her racing heart as if to still it. The curve of his fingers on her breast made breathing all the more precious. Her nipples grew rigid, the one straining to greet his palm.

"Ah, love . . ." He angled his head to catch the slant of the sun, his hand sliding down to her waist.

Western light filled his hair with brilliance, from tones of platinum and silver to honey and wheat. She wanted to feel that head rest on her naked breast while she counted each lustrous strand.

"One miracle at a time, love. We're two hours from tonight's camp. And you're not up to anything that requires heavy breathing."

The rest of the hike that day was companionable and lovely, an enjoyment of the rugged beauty around them. Flowers filled Kyla's braid, a sample of each blossom they came across. Luke would pluck the delicate treasures and thread them into her braid, draping the russet rope over her shoulder.

Each marvelous new discovery countered the fatigue that throbbed with each pull of her legs. Her exhaustion was gratifying, akin, she thought, to the satisfaction of devoting every waking minute to a long-shot sales package and then seeing it go through.

Filling their canteens one last time, they turned away from the stream and headed for dry, high ground. "This is it," Luke finally announced. The clearing was on level land with a thick stand of trees to the east to block the fierce rays of the morning sun.

Kyla collapsed. She didn't know what had suffered more, her legs, her lungs, or her spirit. Luke pulled items from the packs, setting up camp. Kyla knew she should pitch in, planned to . . . eventually. He gathered dead wood and built a fire. He draped a waterproof tarp over a couple of stunted trees, anchoring the corners with rocks. He unrolled both sleeping bags and placed them zipper-to-zipper under the canvas roof. Whenever his eyes fell on Kyla, he smiled. Not only was she unable to force herself to help him, she couldn't even muster up a weak smile in response.

More elegant meals had graced Kyla's table, but she couldn't remember any that had tasted better than the one she balanced on her lap. Bubbling-hot canned stew, pan-fried biscuits that Luke called bannocks—a hiker's staple, he said—and more oranges to restore depleted vitamin C.

The sun set—as gloriously afire as Luke had promised—taking warmth with it. Hugging her knees to her chest, Kyla wrapped her hands around the hot tin of her coffee mug. It didn't calm the shivers in her slim shoulders. She'd already donned every layer of clothing in her pack.

"Here, love." Luke pulled his sweater off and slid it over her head.

"What about you?" More comforting than the thick covering were his scent and body warmth settling around her with the wool.

"I'm fine. Move up closer to the fire."

Sounds of wood life amplified in the dark and were made more menacing by the night. Kyla's body was exhausted, but her imagination was working overtime. When Luke pulled out a length of rope and tied their packs together, Kyla asked him what he was doing.

"Hanging the food to keep it from the grizzlies." He threw one end of the rope over a tree limb ten feet above the ground and then hoisted their packs into the air.

"You're not kidding, are you?" A new emotion to add to her list—dread.

"I'm not kidding."

"Does hanging the food keep them away?"

"No. It keeps them occupied trying to get it down . . . while we run like hell."

The blood in her brain made a beeline for her feet.

"The grizzly is nearly extinct, Kyla. I've never seen one in these parts. However, there are those who have, so I take all precautions. Don't worry, love. We're safe. Now, crawl in the sack before you fall asleep where you sit."

Luke rolled back one corner of her sleeping bag while Kyla kicked out of her cumbersome boots. She eyed the bedroll suspiciously.

"What now?" Luke asked with more than a touch of asperity.

"Shouldn't we check it for rattlesnakes or scorpions?"

"Only in the desert where they crawl in to get out of the sun. Now, get your bottom in there."

The air mattress under her sleeping bag was the softest contact her body had known all day. Luke lay down beside her, ignoring the zippers and drawing up the two downy flaps as if they were one huge blanket. He pulled her into his arms, fitting her against his chest. Kyla gazed over his shoulder, beyond the edge of the tarpaulin roof. "Beautiful. A purple satin sky," she mumbled. "Luke," she whispered.

"Mm-hmm?"

"I . . . well, I figured . . . we'd . . ."

"I know, love. And we will." He chuckled, the sound a velvet glove stroking her senses. "When you're awake and can enjoy it. Now, go to sleep."

Where passionate desire had surged in her veins that afternoon, fatigue now flowed, leaving her numb in its wake. Drifting on clouds of exhaustion, she turned her cheek to the softness of his cotton shirt. "Oh, Luke." She struggled to sit up. "You must be freezing."

"For goodness' sake, Kyla, go to sleep!"

"But I've got your sweater."

"And I've got you. Now, come back to my arms and keep me warm."

Kyla didn't remember another thing until she woke with the dawn, paralyzed by excruciating pain.

"Oh, my Lord," she croaked.

A hulking figure stood at her feet. Squinting, she focused on Luke cloaked in his sleeping bag. "Beginning to feel life, I see. Sore?"

"Shoot me. I'll be forever grateful." She felt as if she'd been staked to the ground with railroad spikes, then set aflame. "I can't get up."

Luke leaned down and with a swift jerk put her on her feet. "You need to move around. Work the knots out."

Her first steps were unbearable. Rolling her shoulders, she forced warm blood into muscles that were frozen stiff. "Smells good," she mumbled, waking to the aroma of hot coffee and pancakes, mingling with the sweet scent of wood smoke.

"Bannock flapjacks," Luke said, flipping the golden cakes.

"Bannock biscuits, bannock flapjacks." The words wheezed out as Kyla stretched fingertips to toes. "Adaptable stuff, this bannock."

"Civilized too. In the real world it's called Bisquick."

Given her druthers, Kyla would have lingered over breakfast all morning.

"Move it, love," Luke urged as he packed up camp. "You've got one helluva day ahead of you."

Kyla narrowed her eyes on him. Why was today so different from yesterday? she wondered. "How so?" He attached the pack to her back and she stumbled to regain her footing. How could it have grown heavier? The consumed food alone should have subtracted some weight.

"The land we cover today is stingy—with water, with beauty. You'll have to look hard to find them. You're going to push and sweat, fall down and get back up to push and sweat again. You're going to ration water or run out. You're going to think the sun is burning you up. and when it's all over, tenderfoot, you'll stand on top of the world."

Nothing in her life had prepared Kyla for the grueling heat and utter exhaustion. Stone and bark bit into her skin, the soles of her feet were on fire, her mouth and throat were coated with grit. Luke was right—she had to look hard to find anything beautiful. But when she did there was no describing the wonder of it: a vine eking out an existence miles from water, dripping soft white blossoms over hot gray rock; a distant mountainside carpeted with lush wildflowers when all around her bare patches of dry scrub struggled to keep roots anchored in dust.

And more marvelous than the discoveries buried in this primitive land were those she unearthed in herself. She'd begun this journey as timid as the satiny flowers, only to grow as determined as the stubborn scrub . . . until—

"No! Absolutely not!" She stood at the jagged edge of earth looking across an abyss to its opposite side, long ago separated by volcanic activity. There was no discernible floor to the river of space, only unending blackness.

Luke tied one end of his rope to his backpack and

one end to a stone that he hurled to the other side. Taking a running start, he hurdled the rift, then hauled his pack over. Kyla noticed that he'd *just* cleared the edge.

"That's how you do it."

"No. That's how *you* do it!"

Leaping back to her side, Luke scratched two lines in the earth the approximate width of the ravine. Packless, Kyla tried over and over to jump the simulated distance. She failed every attempt.

"Damn, you've got short legs." He frowned, thinking. "How is your sense of balance?"

"Forget it." Kyla dropped to the ground, aching with defeat. She had worked so hard to come this far. The pipe dream of making it to the top had crystallized into a very real possibility, and now . . . "If you think you can tie that rope to a tree on either side and make me walk it, think again."

Unsnapping the hatchet from his belt, he surveyed a sparse stand of woods. "A tree. You can walk a tree, hmm? A four-inch trunk should hold a little thing like you."

Kyla watched him take a young tree down, then decapitate its leaves, and was reminded of the day she'd first met him. The powerful swing of his arms, the bunch of chest muscles straining his shirt, the taps filling the air, and the sweat pouring over bronze flesh. Unpending the log, he let it fall, creating a natural bridge across the ravine. "Maple," he murmured sadly. "Beautiful trees in the autumn, maples. Take forever to grow at this altitude."

Oh, great! she fumed. He had just murdered a beloved tree to get her across. How was she supposed to refuse him now? Luke threw her boots and pack to the other side and tied the rope around Kyla's waist—just in case.

When everything, including Luke, was where Kyla had to get to, she offered up a fervent prayer. Luke checked the security of the log on his side, then nodded his head. Fear rose up to surround her in a thick cowardly cloud, no longer her protective walls but a suffocating blanket. Dragging damp palms down her thighs, Kyla stepped onto the horizontal tree. "Don't lose me, Luke."

"Never. Just lock those big brown eyes on mine and keep coming. Don't look down." She did exactly what he told her, her stocking feet inching along the bark. At the point of no return she wavered, and sensed Luke's hands tighten on the rope, ready for her fall.

"I'm . . . I'm dizzy." She could barely breathe.

"Don't close your eyes! Don't look down!" He trusted her. Believed in her. Dared her to fail him now. "Come to me, love. Almost there," he whispered. She never stopped staring into his soft green eyes, letting them pull her across.

Then she fell into his arms. His heart drummed furiously under her ear. His chest heaved as he grabbed a shuddering breath. "You're one helluva lady. Scared to death, but you kept right on coming at me."

From day one, Kyla thought. From the first second she'd laid eyes on him.

"You made it, love. You did it."

His arms were all that held her up. Her knees shook, her bones were melting like candle wax. She'd gone as far as she could. That perch between heaven and death had been her last desperate effort. "I'm done, Luke." She cried the concession into his shirt. Pride at her accomplishment was diminished by not going the distance. "I can't go any farther."

With comforting strokes, his big gentle hand caressed the wild wisps of hair that had escaped her braid. "Think you can manage fifty yards at a gentle rise?" He set her trembling body away from him, actually uncurling her fingers from his belt. He nodded to a slope of land where a single stunted tree grew. "The top, love."

"I made it?" Was it possible she had only to walk the rest of the way? No rocks to trip over? No branches to tear at her face and hair? No ledge to fall from to her death?

"You made it," Luke said. But he spoke the words to her back, for she'd already turned and started on the last leg of her journey. Alone. Alive.

When Luke, lugging her boots and both packs, arrived at the summit, he found her with her face lifted to the sun, her arms stretched open and wide, and standing as tall as any five-feet-even body could.

She smiled over one slim shoulder. "I can see Kansas!"

"An acre of Nevada, maybe."

So beautifully, incredibly rugged, Kyla thought as she turned in circle after circle. They weren't on the highest peak. Others, lofty and broad, sported white caps of snow. Her eyes traveled the winding route of scooped-out valleys forming passes through the western side of the range. The afternoon sun painted pink ribbons behind the highest peaks.

"How do you feel, Kyla?"

She took a deep breath, tracking the passage of crisp air from nostrils to lungs and back again. *How do I feel?* she thought. It mattered that her answer convey how precious his gift was. *How did she feel?* Tired and sweaty. Sore beyond belief. Satisfied. Good. At peace with herself. Meeting his gaze, she blinked at the tears gathering. "Whole. I feel whole."

He reached out, beckoning her with his open hand, with his smile, with his gentle gaze.

"Time to go?" Fingertips touched and curled around each other. Kyla looked up into his stunning face. Sweat streaks lined the dirt, and wood chips from axing the tree clung to his disheveled hair like pale snowflakes. And he was no less beautiful because of it, she marveled.

"Look down there." He curled one arm around her waist. The other indicated a distant patch of green life rimming a blue pond a short hike down the opposite side of the mountain they'd just come up. "Tonight's camp."

She wasn't ready to leave her mountaintop. Her ego and her legs both protested the idea. The shadows of the sole tree called her, and Kyla slumped in the coolness there. "No wonder you love it so, Luke."

"And what do you love?" he asked.

"Me?" She closed her eyes. "I love my job. My three nieces. I love hot fudge sundaes and my temperamental car. A sunny spring day. Thunderstorms. I love baby kittens . . ." Superimposed on the vision of all she loved was Luke. "What do you love? Besides this mountain?"

Only his baritone voice touched her. "My parents. Sky-diving. I love a thick barbecued steak smothered in onions. Little kids on playgrounds. I love a game of touch football with the guys . . . and you."

Heart and lungs stopped. No, he'd said something about playing touch ball with her. She dragged her eyelids up and found Luke standing against the brilliant backdrop of a cloudless sky. "I . . . I don't play football."

"I love you, Kyla." His gaze was steady. "I love you."

Six

I love you.

A thousand moments passed with Kyla unable to move, to think. *I should do something,* she thought desperately. *Say* something. Her pulse rate accelerated in concentrated response while the rest of her petrified. For the first time in her life, restless activity deserted her.

She watched Luke stride to the backpacks and hitch one over each arm, as calmly as if he'd just said "I love tomatoes." His jade eyes met hers in a searching gaze. Strangely, Kyla knew it wasn't reciprocal love he looked for—his smile exemplified confidence.

"If there were a bathroom up here," he said in bittersweet tones, "I believe you'd be locking yourself in right about now." Kyla grabbed a deep breath, the sort to presage a rush of words—but none came. "It's all right, love. I'm going down to make camp. Come when you're ready. It's an easy hike and you're a pro now. You'll manage."

A voice in her head screamed at him to stop, stay, say it again. Her mouth did little more than hang open, incapable of preventing his retreat. Bewildered, Kyla stared at her folded legs, at grubby wool socks on swollen feet, at scratched, dirty hands casually curled around her kneecaps—as if they were foreign objects.

I love you.

She glanced up at the bright azure sky as a rush of warm air enfolded her. *He loves me!* she shouted silently. Elation percolated in her veins. Her heart threatened to burst like a shaken bottle of champagne. She'd assumed her inner turbulence at the mere thought of him was due to fear having declared war on desire—the man pulling one way, consequence the other. She'd been wrong. The security of his love did nothing to calm the turmoil. If anything, the realization that soon she would lie with him, love with him, whipped her senses into a higher frenzy. She was on top of the world and spiraling to heaven.

Scrambling to her feet, she shoved them into the clammy leather of her boots. The trail hugged the mountain's western slope. A fresh breeze drifted up from the small rock-rimmed lake where sunlight splashed diamonds on its glittering surface. Reflected branches framed the collecting pool in delicate lacework.

A wedge of smooth stone overhung the water, and Kyla stood there appreciating the lake's clarity as Luke, submerged and naked, swam by. Powerful muscles rippled sensuously in a fluid, mesmeric wave, from the arms extended past his head to the long, lean legs pressed together.

Stepping back to the treeline, Kyla shed the filthy clothes she'd lived and labored in the last two days. All of them. Her breasts and bottom tingled to the delicious caress of sun and wind. She considered the soft heap of clothes at her feet. They looked lifeless and forlorn. As if the person who'd filled them had vanished—thawed out and melted away.

With untested bravado, she returned to the granite platform, curled her toes over its edge, and waited.

Luke surfaced in the center of the pool and saw her—every alabaster inch of her. He stood in breathless quietude at a depth that exposed most of his bronzed chest. With downcast eyes, Kyla watched her fingers unplait the triple-strand braid, smiling softly. His radiant gaze drew heat from the sun-baked ledge into her ankles and calves, shimmered warmth along her thighs to gather as hot liquid at the juncture of her legs. Peering through the veil of her lashes, she saw him take in the subtle curve of her hips, include the daintily depressed navel and triangle of dark, downy hair. When his fevered gaze lifted to pouting nipples, she raised her hands to her head to rake loose the russet strands of hair.

She made her dive shallow, bracing herself for the shock of her toasty flesh hitting the cool water. Rushing to the surface, she searched for the lake's floor with her toes. Water lapped seductively at her nipples, revealing, then hiding the full coral buds.

"You look surprised to see me," Kyla said. A yard separated them, and she'd expected to be immediately drawn to his hard length. But he didn't move. He barely breathed. "Did you think I'd bolt?"

"The possibility occurred to me." With the languid sweep of one hand, Luke scattered the floating cloud of her hair before it could drift forward to curtain her breasts.

Were they too small? she wondered, not daring to breathe. Why didn't he touch them . . . her? Never before had Kyla so desperately wanted a man to look at her and adore the sight. She, who felt triumph when men appreciated her keen intelligence, didn't care at this moment if every cell in her brain had disintegrated, if only this man would find her body appealing.

A rough breath ripped from her lips. "Am I okay? To . . . to look at?"

"Okay? Lord, love, you're beautiful," he said huskily. "Even more beautiful than I imagined." The boyish dimple graced his cheek. "And I spent a lot of time imagining."

Relief filled her next breath as she moved her flame-struck eyes from his deep green ones to the carved, sensuous mouth. Water beaded on his broad shoulders and drifted into the gold filaments matting his chest.

"Don't you want to hold me . . . or . . . or something?"

A choked groan answered her. Then he offered a soft curse to the sky. "Love, if I held you now, I'd crush you. I'd take you too fast, too rough. Do you know what you just did to me? Standing there all of a sudden? So small and perfect? And, Lord, so beautiful?"

Something primitive and just a bit savage magnetized the air, as it had the first time she'd seen him. She'd forgotten how raw and powerful that feeling was. He'd been so tender and considerate, getting her up the mountain. But he wouldn't be, in passion. And, Kyla realized, she didn't want him to be.

"I put shampoo and soap out for you." He inclined his head and Kyla glanced over to see the coveted articles on a stone ledge. "While you bathe, I'm going to set up a fish trap I leave here. Then I'll be ready to spend the rest of the afternoon with you."

Sinking under the water, he swam away. Kyla waded to shallower depths where the meager toilet articles waited. He could spend all the time he wanted in this cool water, she decided, bridling his passion. But Luke, of all people, wasn't going to cheat her of the very unleashed passion he had encouraged her to crave.

She'd washed her hair and was reaching for the soap when Luke returned. Splashing sounds circled her from behind until he stood in front of her, their difference in height blatantly obvious. Calm water screened Kyla from below her navel. Luke was gloriously exposed. She caught her breath and raptly gazed at his virile manhood.

"Will it bother you if I stay?" he asked softly.

Kyla shook her head. "No." Trembling fingers touched the small white cake.

"Ah, love, let me." He lifted the soap from her loose grip as he drew her back into his arms. "Do you know how long I've wanted to feel you against me?" His thick, low voice poured into her veins. "Without buttons or blouses or those unbreachable jeans between us. Just skin . . . on skin." He massaged her waist and soft belly. "And I don't have a single civilized thought in my head."

Kyla shivered as he drew circles on her rib cage in increasingly higher sweeps, dispensing frothy suds over satin skin. "Neither do I," she whispered, "Nothing remotely civil."

Drugging pleasure closed her eyes as his hands performed a sweet bathing of her breasts. "You're not too small for me here, love."

She leaned back, boldly inviting his eyes to watch the magic he worked. Narrow runnels of lacy bubbles rolled from her breasts. Luke's eyes traced the delicate trails as if each were a drop of whipped cream and at any moment he would swoop down and lap up the sweet rivers with his tongue. He soaped her breasts until her slippery nipples refused to stay pinched in his fingers. Each impudent escape of the aroused tips sent a shaft of desire darting to the lower regions of her body.

"Don't stop, Luke." She practically cried the words when his hands sank back to the water.

"I won't, love. I won't." Scooping cool water, he carried it to her shoulder and released a rinsing trickle. Again and again, until her flesh shone like polished ivory.

Brushing his flattened hand along her hips, he swept down her thigh underwater, coming back up slowly. The smooth bar in his palm preceded the rasp of slightly rough fingers and the gentle rake of his nails.

At the request of his fingers, she parted her legs. Dipping forays to the secret silken warmth sent rippling shivers on a course that left her weak. Kyla sobbed a soft pleasurable cry.

"This is hell, love. Standing in an ice bath and touching you. The spirit sends one message, the flesh another."

She turned in his embrace, lifting her arms to his shoulders, and her lips to his mouth. The kiss was fierce, a dueling of lips and tongues accompanied by a love harmony of feminine purrs and masculine growls praising the ardent mating.

Luke scooped her up in his arms. Water rushed from her pale flesh in silver streams. A set of graduated stones formed a natural staircase and he carried her out of the pond. He lowered his head to lay a worshipful kiss at her tiny waist and sip the moisture puddled there.

Kyla sighed. "Oh, Luke. I wanted to be so beautiful for you."

"You are, love. My little bit of wild beauty." He lifted a water bead from her cheek with his lips. "Wishing you hadn't pitched your makeup, hmm?"

Setting her on her feet, he backed away. Kyla loved the smooth grace of his naked body, the unaffected ease with which he strode about the small paradise, neither shy nor arrogant. Broad shoulders tapered to lean waist. The small of his back hollowed gently to ride firm buttocks. Ropes of muscle modeled his thighs and calves with a power that still made Kyla shiver.

Pinching off two vines crowded with tiny blue flowers, he brought them to her. After securing one in her hair, he looped and tied the other around her neck. Tears welled in her eyes as he gently adorned her with the delicate beauties of his world. Dewy satin petals lay on the high swell of her breasts, teasing them into readiness for a fiercer caress.

"I love you, Luke." Her dark gaze sparkled with joy and wonder. "I love you."

"Damn those eyes," he muttered. "Say the words that fill them. What do they plead for?"

"For you. Love me, Luke. Love me now."

He pulled her down to the cool grass, pressing his hard length to her side. Their mouths came together, his tongue slipping past her lips with a gentle probe that belied the consequent plundering. He tasted, approved, and devoured.

His mouth trailed heat over her throat and shoulders, encountering the cool flowers. He nudged them away with his nose, uncovering the nipple his mouth sought. Sweet ecstasy rushed through her as his hot tongue lashed the aroused peak. He painted her breasts with the moisture of his mouth, then suckled her with tender insistence. Kyla gazed lovingly at his blond head, at her breast plumped out by his sweet nuzzling. And she knew that while he fed from her, he nurtured her soul.

"You taste so good," Luke murmured over a groan. "You *feel* so good." Places she would never have thought erogenous became so under his touch. The shell of her ear, the nape of her neck, the inside of her wrist. He placed a stinging kiss in the palm of her hand, then carried her fingers over his face, dragging her soft imprint across his jaw to his mouth. He watched her eyes widen and glaze as he pulled the tips of her fingers into his mouth and drew on them.

And then he watched her eyes close as his hands stole to the silky flesh of her thighs, urging her legs to part. A sizzle ripped over her nerves at his first inquisitive touch. Her eyes flew open when he closed his hand over her, pressing circles into the throbbing heat with the heel of his palm. Circles that moved into her hips, driving waves of pleasure into her veins.

"Luke," she breathed.

"Feel life, love," he urged. "It'll be perfect. Feel it." His fingers curled inward and up, and life was a crashing, brilliant explosion. Her pores expanded to capture the thrill as it raced over her skin. Life tore at her muscles and sent a white-hot excitement through her soul and heart.

Forcing her blurred vision to focus on Luke's face, she lifted a surprisingly heavy hand to touch her fingers to his smiling lips. On a path that gave equal pleasure, her hand drifted down his throat, through curled chest hair to satin skin. Curving her fingers to Luke's waist, she relished the lean flare of his hip on her palm. A sweep to the smooth ridge of bone elicited a sucking gasp from Luke. His mouth hovering over hers pulled the breath from her body into his lungs. Tracing the satin arrow of gold hair below his navel, she reached for the hardness of him.

"Ah, love . . . easy . . ." His labored pants echoed the caresses of her hand. "I'll loss control, tenderfoot. Easy, love."

Kyla combed the crisp fur on his chest with her other hand, each stroke calculated to impassion. "Lose control," she begged. "Don't cheat me, Luke."

His eyes swept over her. "So perfect," he said in awe. "So small."

Burying her hands in his tawny mane, she drew his eyes back to hers. "And strong, Luke. You made me strong. Come love me . . . now . . . now." She drew him over her, rising to the thrill of sinewed flesh and steely heat.

"Make me gentle, love." Sinking to his knees on the ground between her legs, he let his weight come to her slowly. The finesse of his mouth bathed her with soft warmth. Love melted through her and she lifted her hips to him. Kyla reached to guide him, urging his entrance with a surety that ripped the tethers he'd placed on his passion. Plunging deeply, he buried himself in the damp silk and gripping love of her. Her nails sank into the flesh of his shoulders and a sweet, ecstatic cry left her lips.

"Did I hurt you?" Luke froze, gasping moist pants at her ear.

"No, it's good . . . so good . . ."

"Oh, Lord . . ." he groaned, and drove deeper. The colors of paradise filled Kyla, gathering, then splintering. Fragrances assaulted her senses, the perfumes of earth and skin and being alive.

"Luke, Luke . . ." It became her chant, exhaled on the crest of each passionate wave. With a sharp cry, Luke joined and became the impetus of her ecstasy. Not only whole, was her last thought, but complete.

Kyla lay curled to Luke's side. His muscular arm pillowed her head, while his hand moved lazily on her hips. She inhaled his clean male scent. His naked flesh treated her to a variety of textures from hard and rough to smooth and soft. Were her tastebuds as sensitive to the physical? she wondered. Avid to satisfy her curiosity, she stroked his bare shoulder with her tongue. Tangy, sharp. Everything in the physical world had a new intensity for her.

Shivers raced over her skin when Luke reciprocated her damp nuzzles on the sensitive spot just behind her ear. She squirmed in his arms and he moaned with the pleasure her wriggling gave him.

"Only an hour of daylight left, tenderfoot." His voice sent a new wave of shivers down her body. "And much to do yet."

The sun had dissolved to a red stain in the sky overhead. "Like get dressed," Kyla managed through chattering teeth.

Luke stood as Kyla sat up. Leaning down, he combed through her hair, shaking loose a confetti shower of crushed blue flowers. Sometime during their lovemaking her delicate necklace had been torn away and lay scattered in the grass.

They dressed hastily, the cold attacking hands and feet first and rushing quickly inward. On a devilish impulse, Kyla left her bra and panties tucked in the bottom of her pack. Her soft brown corduroys and cozy flannel shirt slipped over her bare flesh with a feeling of more decadence than satin bedsheets.

Luke left to check the trap, returning with his fist wrapped around a tail-flapping fish. "Dinner," he proclaimed, proudly holding his trophy up for inspection.

Kyla threw one arm out in a traffic-stopping gesture. The other hand she clapped over her eyes. "Don't introduce us! Just behead and . . . and decimate in private. Bury the evidence. I'll pretend you've just come from the market with plastic-wrapped fillets."

Intent on ignoring the slaughter—and Luke's inappropriate laughter as he performed it—Kyla wandered back to the path leading to the mountaintop. Birds sang a farewell litany to the dying sun while Kyla sat, cradling her knees to her chest, on the edge of the world and the brink of a new, expanded life.

In the last moments of the day, she heard his footsteps and gazed over her shoulder at his graceful, prowling approach. Lord, how she loved him!

Crouching behind her, he pulled her between his bent knees, fitting her back to his chest. "What are you thinking?" he asked quietly.

"I'm wondering if I qualify as a physical person."

His chuckle was soft and deep. "You qualify, love. A definite graduate. Magna cum laude."

In silence they watched the sun slip away, until there were only enough rays to light the way down.

"You're right," Kyla said, licking the last drip of butter from her fingertips. "I hadn't tasted trout until you cooked it." They cuddled in the glow of the campfire under the mantle of a sleeping bag, protected from the wind by a crevice in the rock wall.

"Full?" he asked, lifting her chin.

"Mmm." Kyla sighed. "Very full."

"Tired?"

"A little tired." She yawned and giggled. "More than a little."

"Happy?"

"Happy?" She narrowed her eyes in contemplation. "I don't know about happy."

His fingers worked deftly to undo her first three buttons. "Can't have that." Easing the material to one side, he exposed her warm, soft breast to the cold air. "Why, Ms. Trent, where the hell is your underwear?"

His thumb grazed her nipple as Kyla set her features in demure shyness. "I'm not wearing any."

"None?"

"None."

"Becoming a savage little thing, aren't you?" He kissed her neck, then lifted her breast with an adoring hand, enveloping her nipple with his seeking lips.

Kyla drew the downy blanket around them while Luke made her sublimely happy.

They were rambunctious, playful lovers coming down the mountain the next day. Hungry, devoted lovers in Luke's cabin Saturday night. Quiet, wistful lovers when it was time for Kyla to leave the mountains on Sunday.

Luke slammed the door of her little car. The hollow thump echoed in Kyla's heart. "Drive carefully, love," he ordered, sticking his head through the open window to kiss her good-bye. "I'll be back in L.A. next week. I'll call." He patted his breast pocket where the paper with her address and phone number rested.

Kyla pulled out of the rutted drive wondering how she'd survive the seven days without him.

Seven

The irony of unveiling Opticillusion, Visionary Tech's newest computer line, in a hotel dripping Victorian opulence, paralleled San Francisco's integration of old and new—a town where tall, sleek skyscrapers cast long shadows on whimsical gingerbread homes. Throughout the city, that fanciful confusion had been lovingly preserved.

Vince Hawthorne, CampuMart's general sales manager, and Bill Danvers, regional manager, finished registering and departed for the double they would share. Mutt and Jeff, Kyla thought with a smile, watching Vince, a squat cigar-chewer, waddle away, with Bill, a lanky stringbean, ambling beside him. She waited while Andrew Carson completed the necessary billing forms, scanning the weekend's product-seminar agenda. She had decided to skip Sunday's promotional itinerary and fly home after the technical instructions tomorrow.

It had been a whirlwind week, a gratifying, exhilarating week. Recalled, the last five days were a blur of activity, beginning with Kyla's move to the vice-president's office and interspersed with late-night planning sessions. She'd expected a certain authority and new responsibilities to go with the extra square-footage and thicker pile carpeting. But Andrew had staggered Kyla by practically handing over the reins and climbing into the passenger seat.

"I'm sixty-four and I'm tired," Andrew had grumbled after one late session in the office. They were alone in the slumbering quiet and had just closed the files for the night. "My wife talks about the vegetable garden I'll tend when I retire. The bird feeders I'll build. I can take up watercolors and 'won't *that* be nice.' " He'd rolled his eyes expressively and Kyla had laughed softly into the comfortable silence.

"I wouldn't survive the retirement. I want to come in at ten and go home at two. Hand out the Christmas bonus. Give an occasional gold watch. Sit front row center while you direct the show.

"Hell, it's a baby's industry. You'll fit, Kyla. I don't anymore."

Now, as Andrew finished with the concierge, a smooth voice called out, "Mr. Carson, Ms. Trent." They turned as one to see a man with brown hair and brown eyes, neatly tucked into a brown suit, moving briskly through the lavish clutter of the lobby. His face was unfamiliar, but Kyla recognized the perfectly trained voice from their extensive telephone negotiations.

He introduced himself in a series of abrupt, concise titles. "Bob Christman. Visionary Tech. Vice-president of sales." He pumped Andrew's hand, then annoyed Kyla by feminizing the gesture with a light grasp of her fingertips. "Congratulations, Ms. Trent, on your recent promotion." His smile involved no more of his face than necessary. What's going on? Kyla wondered. Manufacturers didn't grin and bear distributors. "All checked-in? Good, good. I'll walk with you to your rooms."

An elevator yawned open and Christman waited

for its enclosed privacy before dropping his bomb. "The Quantum management team will be attending the seminar this weekend. We're bringing them on the line." No blow-softening lead-in. Nor, Kyla noted caustically, even a pretense of apology for the breach of trust.

She swallowed a burst of anger and glanced at Andrew. His only reaction was a surprised lift of his brows. *Your baby*, his silence said. *And it just slipped under the bathwater. Save it!* A soft bump and the elevator opened on the second floor. Andrew strode out. Christman moved two paces to the "open-door" button and depressed it for Kyla's exit. End of the line. Perfect timing.

Equal parts of intuition and experience warned Kyla that if she let this elevator carry Bob Christman away, he'd be "unavailable" for the balance of the seminar. Sliding her hands into the pockets of her full, fawn-colored cashmere skirt, Kyla looked the man straight in his unreadable brown eyes. "Your firm—*you*—promised us exclusivity, Mr. Christman. We committed to handle a million in sales the first year, based on that promise. Now you're telling us you've brought on a competitor?"

His return gaze matched hers in directness. The ball was in his court. It occurred to Kyla he just might take it and go home. "I assure you, this all happened quite suddenly. This morning, in fact. Opticillusion is a tremendously hot item. Our marketing people outdid themselves in generating excitement. Mr. Morainge, Quantum's president, has indicated a market penetration CompuMart can't possibly meet."

If it's such a hot little item, Kyla thought acidly, we damn well *can* meet it. "What'll it take to get exclusivity written in the contract?"

Genuine surprise slapped a little life into Christman's wax-figure face. "A million-five might have wrapped it last week. Now . . ." He shrugged, implying it was hopeless.

The "open-door" buzzer sounded. Kyla glanced at it casually. She was in no hurry. "A number, Bob. A solid number."

"Commit two million the first year, my company will write it in the contract."

Double! Morainge's deal with Visionary grew more devastating by the minute. Four West Coast distributors were scheduled to attend this product seminar, she recalled, all from noncompetitive territories: Washington, Oregon, San Francisco, and Compu-Mart's Los Angeles/San Diego region. Had Quantum contracted to match all four dollar for dollar? A few? Or only CompuMart?

"Arrange a meeting for me with your sales team." Kyla stepped into the hallway. "Shall we say eight o'clock tomorrow morning in the coffee shop?"

An answer wasn't expected. Kyla's back and the door sighing shut didn't allow one. She purposely let him believe she would consider the option. Buying time. At these prices, time was all CompuMart could afford!

She found her room, stabbing the lock with her key. Two million! A swift kick slammed the door behind her. Rapid taps on the interconnecting door echoed the ache beginning behind her eyes. Slipping out of her heels, she padded barefoot across thick blue carpeting to let Andrew in.

"What happened?" he asked.

"That's exactly what I'd like to know! We had verbal exclusivity."

"Which is as binding as the paper it wasn't written on." He sighed with mild resignation, navigating the imitation Queen Anne furniture to reach a set of French doors. He threw them open, stepping onto the second-floor veranda overlooking lush gardens. "First time for us that a manufacturer didn't stand by an oral commitment. But it happens."

"You're taking this surprisingly well," Kyla said. "We've made a frightening commitment that *is* binding. The only way Quantum can make their quota is by unloading one hell of a lot of *their* units on clients *we* need."

"I am not taking it well, Kyla. I am simply taking it. And I expect you will take care *of* it." Andrew watched her through the open doors—a disciplined whirlwind conversely creating order. She transferred clothes from the suitcase to a dresser drawer with one hand, plucked the pins from her hair with the other. A drawer was bumped shut by a hip, another opened, and the lamp turned on. Hanging clothes were dashed to the closet. She ducked into the bathroom to start hot water in the shower with a spin of the taps. Stow suitcase, peel off and hang jacket, adjust air conditioner. All in less than five minutes.

"You've always put together our most lucrative deals in make-or-break situations. It's the reason I promoted you over Myers and Upton. They're great salesmen. But you . . . you sit on the edge of disaster and swing your feet. It's the best seat in the house as far as you're concerned."

"What did I ever do to you to deserve such faith?" Kyla complained lightly.

"And you're cheap," Andrew quipped, wandering back into the room. "You pack a twenty-hour workload into a ten-hour day. Two for the price of one."

Kyla laughed. It felt good. The blow had been dealt, absorbed, and Andrew was right—the adrenaline greased her creative wheels.

"Visionary is hosting a private dinner party tonight," Andrew said from his door. "I'll call for you at seven."

Alone, Kyla stripped and hopped in the shower, letting the scalding spray pummel her body. The minute she touched the slim cake of hotel soap, she thought of Luke. It happened every time. Only five days, and she yearned for him as if it had been five thousand. The frenzy at the office this week was all that had kept her from leaping in her car and heading back to the mountains. Monday. Monday he would be back in Los Angeles. Monday she would be back in his arms.

Kyla slipped the last hairpin into her twisted braid and double-checked the coiled figure eight at the back of her head with a hand mirror. Hair and makeup met with a nod of approval in the bathroom's wall mirror—and that was saying a lot considering the fluorescent light's fault-finding glare.

In the bedroom, prismed lamplight shimmered in her white silk dress, transforming the fabric to a drape of liquid pearl. The sleeves were long, the neck high, and a wide gold belt cinched her waist. Tasteful, soft, simple, she thought. Kyla didn't imitate menswear in her clothes to imply authority as so many women in business seemed to do. Expertise had nothing to do with a blue serge suit, and sophisticated flair often spoke volumes, she felt.

At precisely seven o'clock, Andrew knocked at her door. Vince and Bill waited for them at the elevator, looking grim. Kyla assumed Andrew had filled them in on the Quantum hitch. By tacit agreement, discussion of CompuMart's business was avoided in the public areas of the hotel. The attending firms had been housed on different floors but that hardly assured privacy in halls or elevators.

Five tables for eight were elegantly set with gleaming cutlery in the intimate velvet-draped dining room. Each four-member distribution team would dine with four Visionary reps. Kyla circulated during the cocktail hour, enjoying meeting her colleagues. She was social by nature, thriving on the stimulation of diverse personalities. But small talk was only part of it. Always on the lookout for talented, experienced salespeople, Kyla used any opportunity where the best in the business gathered to add to her mental file drawer. The computer industry grew faster than universities could turn out qualified personnel, and she knew the most fertile ground to harvest often proved to be your neighbor's field.

During a lull, Andrew strolled over and muttered under his breath near her ear, "The Quantum contingent."

Looking up, she caught his nod toward the entrance. She carried her wineglass to her lips, casting a sideways glance at the door. A cluster of dark suited men stood in the entry involved in the ritual of arrival. There were . . . Kyla froze, staring wide-eyed over the rim of etched crystal. One head rose above the others. One head with a mane of luxuriant blond hair. One head of stunning, savage beauty. Luke!

Lord, she'd missed him. And there he stood, as breathtakingly sexy as ever. Her heart experienced a weightless uplifting at the sight of him, then a strange, heavy-handed pressure. *The Quantum contingent.* And Andrew was speaking again. "Lucien Morainge is the tall one."

Lucien Morainge. Lucien Morainge. Kyla couldn't tear her eyes away. And while some obscure compartment in her brain, consigned to collect and pour forth trivia, offered up the theory that everyone in the world had a double, her heart knew the truth. Luke. Lucien. *Her Luke Hudson was Quantum's Lucien Morainge.*

"The blond, Andrew? The tall blond?" Was that her voice? she wondered. So calm and steady? A conveniently available chair back came under her strangling grip. She still held her wineglass tightly. She sipped at it, hoping to pierce the gathering numbness before Andrew asked about her deathly pallor . . . or she fainted. And not once did her tortured stare stray from an unsuspecting Luke. *He lied,* she thought with fury and sorrow. *About his name, about his life. About everything. He lied to me . . . and then he made love to me.*

Bill Danvers and the Oregon group diverted

Andrew with a debate on the latest in securing computer access. Kyla felt distanced from her colleagues.
Voices reached her from down a long tunnel—tinny,
hollow syllables without meaning. Luke moved into
the room, as smooth and untouchable as light flowing through a window, allowing others to come to
him.

He doesn't belong here. The words bounced
around her brain. No matter that they accept him,
she thought, he doesn't belong here—without the
sun in his hair, firelight on his face. She couldn't find
the heart-stopping smile, nor a clue it had ever been,
in the firmly set mouth. His glorious gold mane lay in
soft obedience, as if it had been styled with a blow
dryer. The charcoal fabric of his vested suit molded
his broad body with tailored perfection. He was so . . .
so *civilized.* The eyes, the warm jade eyes she remembered, were cold emeralds when he lifted them from
the man he was speaking to.

He had the blunt, caged look of a lion behind
bars, Kyla decided. *An eagle with his wings clipped.*

The shock of finding him in this room doubled
that of the morning she'd found him in her bed. And
something beautifully special about the future began
to shrivel. The joyful anticipation of Monday began to
slip from her grasp.

His gaze swept the room—a methodical canvass-
ing—passing over Kyla, halting, then backing up. He
stared, without welcome or joy. No thirst slaked in
those eyes while drinking her in. *He hasn't missed
me,* she thought. That emotionless scrutiny produced an agony so sharp it nearly severed her sanity.

Keeping his eyes on Kyla, he spoke to a man
whose back was turned to her. The man glanced over
his shoulder before responding.

Grimness lined Luke's mouth as he cocked his
head to consider her across the room. Suddenly
aware she still held the sipped mouthful of wine on
her tongue, she swallowed. Her throat convulsed to

force the bitter liquid into a stomach that had balled into an unaccepting knot.

He began shouldering his way through the room. The hair, the clothes, the eyes might not belong to the Luke she remembered. But the walk—the graceful, prowling approach—that was Luke's. The urge to bolt overwhelmed her; her cultivated sense of survival provoked a feeble one-step retreat. Her withdrawal alerted Andrew and Bill, and so they looked up to see Luke only a few feet away.

Not here, her mind cried out. Suddenly the gravity of her situation crashed in on her. A brain that had refused to assimilate information moments ago bombarded her with disjointed messages. Feelings raced before reason. *My lover is the competition. Unethical. It's happened again. Oh, Lord, he lied to me. I loved him. He* used *me.*

"It's been a while, Andrew." Luke spoke first, shaking hands with the older man. The baritone sound melted through her skin, surged in her veins. "Vegas, wasn't it? The conference two years ago?"

"I believe so, Luke. Have you met my regional manager, Bill Danvers?" Then Andrew turned to his left to introduce Kyla. Could they tell she wasn't breathing? she wondered. "And my vice-president, Kyla Trent."

"What happened to Frank Hooper?" Luke asked, neatly avoiding affirmation or denial to having met Kyla before. Met! Dear Lord in heaven, they'd slept together!

"He retired, Mr. Morainge." Kyla barely managed to utter his name civilly. He offered his hand, and she both feared and wanted his touch. His flesh enveloped hers in warmth, and for the first time the contact brought her pain instead of delirious happiness.

Andrew watched them, misconstruing the palpable tension as the more obvious adversity of business foes. "Christman mentioned you'd be here, Morainge," he said quietly.

The relaxing grip of his hand clamped down at Andrew's comment, crushing Kyla's slim fingers. When she tried to ease her hand free, Luke exerted painful pressure on the fan of delicate bones under his thumb. "You knew."

"You might say I've been waiting for you," Kyla hid sharp heartache behind flat humor.

"Know why I'm here?" His brow lifted over an insolent gaze.

She feigned wide-eyed anticipation. "Don't tell me. A change of scenery?" Andrew and Bill turned back to the other discussion, and she tried again to tug her hand out his grip, and failed.

Luke slid a scorching gaze over her. Slowly, very slowly. His eyes caressed the tempestuous wisps of hair about her face, stroked the silk molding her breasts, skimmed the curve of hip to hem, and traveled over taupe-hosed legs to the strappy high heels she had a penchant for wearing.

"I sure as hell like the scenery so far." His was not a sweet visual stripping but an insulting rape. "Put 'er down, Kyla," he ordered in a soft, deadly tone.

His arrogance sent her chin up in defiance.

"I said, put 'er down." His foot connected with the chair, bumping the seat to the vulnerable backs of her knees. She folded. Her drop to the cushion was inelegant to say the least. Wine sloshed from her glass to the tablecloth and Kyla stared at the expanding stain as Luke settled in the chair beside her.

"Vice-president." His disdain snapped her head up. "*Very* hard ball with *very* big boys." So that was it, she thought. He'd expected Hooper. And, for whatever reason, her unexpected presence angered him.

"And *very* good at it too." With hideous self-loathing, Kyla admitted the likelihood that her weekend in the mountains had been a setup. Logistics—and Kyla was an expert at numbers—made coincidence damned unlikely. That two people, out of billions, would vacation on the same mountain, out of thousands, in one week out of fifty-two, and later turn out to be competitors, was supremely suspect, if circumstantial. That Jerry Bowers, a top-drawer CompuMart salesman, lured away from Quantum six months ago, had gone out of his way to describe the mountain cabin in tempting detail, corroborated the evidence. That Luke lied about his name sent the gavel down on the verdict. She'd have known the name Morainge—everyone in the computer industry did.

He'd manipulated her. But why?

When she closed her eyes, she only found him again, indelibly etched in her mind. Sweat glossy on his skin. Sunlight radiant in his hair. Naked power. Fluid grace. Lord, how could she still want him? The chase, so persistent and seductive, had nothing to do with instant attraction pawned off as love at first sight. And she'd bought it, as naive about the man as she'd been about his mountain. It had all been a scheme. But as wholly as pain filled her heart, Luke still filled her soul.

Facing him, she lifted brown eyes aglitter with anguish. "Go away, Luke. Leave me alone."

"Damn those eyes," he growled. Then, when she thought he would say something else, a Visionary representative arrived and private conversation became impossible. The man wanted Luke to meet someone. He stood and pushed his chair back up to the table. "See you soon, Kyla."

But this time Kyla hoped never to see him again.

Moonlight washed an opal patchwork through the French doors. Kyla lay on the lacy bedspread, staring at the stucco swirls on the ceiling. She had stemmed the tears hours ago, but the visions were ceaseless, her mind a slide projector snapping frame after frame of the evening. Luke had hovered on the edge of her vision through the rest of the cocktail hour. Her eyes shot away if he glanced at her. When he didn't, she absorbed him. The first flash of brilliant smile sang in her blood. What had sparked it? A lofty compliment? A ribald joke? Her eyes followed the rake of lean-boned fingers through his hair, returning it to silken tangles.

Quantum's table was situated directly behind the man across from Kyla. While she'd sampled her salad, its dressing about as appetizing as liquid chalk, Luke had ignored his, smoking one cigarette after another. When the entrée was served, Luke had left the private party and hadn't returned the rest of the evening.

Immediately after she said good night to Andrew and closed her door, the tears had flowed freely. None of it made sense. What had Luke hoped to gain? Damn the soft, seductive gazes veiling deception. Heartbreaking sobs ebbed to the fragile weeping of grief. From dreams woven of joy and fulfillment, there now remained only disillusioned shreds. When the flood of tears subsided, tenacious memories lingered. Laughter on a mountainside. Ecstasy at the summit. Passion in paradise. How could it not have been real?

Rolling over, Kyla glanced at the bedside clock. Two-thirty! And she had a breakfast meeting with the Visionary people. What was she going to say to them? If she let desperation double her commitment, they'd laugh in her face. If she bargained bravely, only to accept the situation meekly, they'd laugh behind her back. She could always call Christman at seven and cancel. The very thought rankled. There had to be something, *something*, that would help her . . . and hurt Luke. As retaliation it was about as effective as an eyelash for an eye.

Too restless to sleep, Kyla slid off the bed and slipped into a long silk robe. She belted the apricot wrap over her thin nightgown and opened the French doors. The balcony passed by all the guest rooms, but at this hour of the morning, she was alone. From here she gazed out at San Francisco sleeping under an ethereal fog. She rested her forehead on a cool pillar and closed her eyes. Love conquers all, she thought dismally—even wounded love. Hers rose above the pain, survived the betrayal. But it hurt . . . it hurt so much.

"Kyla." He whispered her name. "Open your eyes, love, I'm down here."

Thick, dark lashes flew up. Luke stood directly below her, his jacket casually slung over his shoulder, his vest unbuttoned. The knot of his tie rode low on his white shirt, which was open at the throat and rolled up at the sleeves.

Perfection, she thought. The thrill of primitive power barely contained by elegant tailoring. Kyla yearned to pull the sophisticated man to her bed and untether the passionate savage. "Don't you 'love' me," she ordered, her voice thickening with fresh tears. "Go away."

She began to retreat, backing up until her shoulders met the hotel's brick facade. Squeezing her eyes shut, she prayed he wouldn't lean too heavily on her newly made barriers.

"I do love you. I am destined to love you." Like thin ice under a great weight, the brittle cracking began. "We have to talk."

"Are you crazy?" she hissed in a stage whisper. "Andrew has the room next to mine. He'll hear you."

"Then you'd better get down here," he threatened with a rise in pitch. "Or we'll sure as hell wake him if I have to yell up to you."

Kyla lunged at the balustrade and leaned over to glare at him. Waves of dark, wild hair spilled down the lacy ironwork. "Shut up! You've already ruined my life, do you have to ruin my career as well?"

"Ah, love," he murmured. "That's why we need to talk." He gazed up, all the soft understanding of the mountains there in his face.

"So you can tell me more lies?"

"We're going to shout, then?"

"No, we aren't going to speak at all." She whirled away, heading for the sanctuary of her room.

"If you hide behind that door, I'll have to come up *there* and shout."

He will, Kyla realized. He'll do exactly that. "Let me get dressed. Then I'll come down."

"One minute. Then I'll come up."

It would take the whole minute just to strip . . . and that wasn't how she wanted Luke to find her. After sliding her cold feet into slippers, she tied her hair back in a loose ponytail with a thin satin ribbon. Hardly her office bun, but taming the mass always provided some psychological support.

She couldn't go through the lobby in night-clothes so she stepped back onto the balcony and tip-toed to a set of steps at the far end. Luke waited at the bottom of the stairs. When she reached the slate stones of the garden path, Kyla turned away from him. He caught her around the waist from behind and brought her close to his hard length. He nuzzled her neck, his breath flowing down the deep V of her robe. Kyla stiffened in his arms.

"I never lied to you, love," Luke murmured.

She pushed his arms down. "We can be seen here."

Her fingers were interlaced with his. A small tug-of-war took place over her hand until Kyla grew irritated with the adolescent behavior. She sighed and let him lead her down the path through bright azalea bushes dewed by the fog. Behind a stand of high trees sat an old fashioned gazebo. Under the confection of its canopy, they chose opposites sides, then neither seemed to know where or how to start.

Kyla finally broke the silence. "So what do I call you? Luke or Lucien?"

He shrugged. "Whatever you prefer. I answer to both."

"I prefer bastard. Do you answer to that?"

Moonlight flashed on the bunched muscles of his jaw. "Mm-hmm. I've been called it enough."

"I'll just bet you have," Kyla drawled.

Mournful foghorns from the bay echoed through the shifting mist. And Kyla was sure that if her heart could moan, that was the sorrowful keening it would emit.

Luke reached in his breast pocket and pulled out a cigarette. "You're wrong, you know." He tossed his suit jacket to a wrought-iron chair, relegating it to a wrinkled heap. "Men do look at you the way I do. You just don't notice." He exhaled a cloud of smoke that hung in the haze before dissipating. "I watched them tonight. Your diffidence turns them off faster than any words could. They look after you with regret."

Kyla laced her fingers together in front of her and focused on them. Not even in retrospect could she picture the male interest he spoke of.

Then he continued in a low voice, not looking at, but beyond her. "I've been walking the streets tonight, trying to figure this out. I don't have all the pieces yet, but it's beginning to fall together. First, there's Jerry Bowers—" At her gasp, Luke nodded. "I thought so. He told you about the cabin, didn't he?"

Careful, Kyla, she warned herself. You don't *know* he walked the streets. You don't know *what* he's up to. "And you didn't ask him to."

"You think I arranged it? For heaven's sake, Kyla, I didn't even know you until you turned around on Pop's porch. When I was in L.A. three weeks ago, Frank Hooper was sitting at your desk. Can you imagine my shock when I walked into that room tonight and saw you? Do you know what I thought? You told me you distributed medical equipment. First, I thought you were there with someone else . . . one of the salesmen. Then some Visionary rep tells me you're the vice-president of a company I've been looking into—"

"What? Looking into CompuMart? Why?"

"I'll get to that." He dropped his cigarette and ground it beneath his heel. "We're only going to get more confused if we don't go at this one piece at a time. First question: How does a pint-sized woman, wearing Rodeo Drive boots, calling an ax a woodpecker, wind up in Barry Michaels's mountain cabin? Answer: I put Jerry Bowers onto it when he worked for me . . . and now he works for you."

"Yes, he told me about it," Kyla conceded, playing her cards close to her chest. A chest beneath which her heart raced frantically. Luke was looking into her company. Luke had seriously damaged her deal with Visionary just that morning. "I . . . I said I *used* to sell medical equipment . . . in Chicago."

"And you were doing the same thing in California. You meant distribution, but I had no way of knowing that."

"I . . . uh . . ." Kyla couldn't remember her exact words, but Luke's summary certainly seemed plausible. "So you walked into the party tonight and figured . . . what?"

"That you'd come to the mountains to use your feminine talents on me—"

"Because that's how women succeed in business, isn't it! Not with intelligence or experience or training. With allure and sexual favors." Her fury so consumed her, she failed to wonder what he thought she was supposed to have gained from the barter. "Why ever did you change your mind?" she drawled caustically.

He chuckled softly. "You mean besides the fact that I spent far too much time looking at your fanny while you ran the wrong way?" The inquisitive lift of his brow was ignored. "You never talked about your work, and you never really questioned me about mine. I was standing on Nob Hill tonight about to go into the Mark Hopkins for a drink when I remembered Jerry. That's when I came back here to find you." Inclining his head, he narrowed his eyes.

"You've been in the computer business for a long time, Kyla. You'd have recognized my name when we met. Why didn't you say something?" Suspicion made his voice abrasive, a flint to the angry fires Kyla struggled to keep under control.

"I was supposed to know Luke Hudson of the mountains was Lucien Morainge of Quantum Company?" she snapped back.

He groaned, a sound that swelled into a vicious expletive hurled at the sky. "Hudson. Luke Hudson. I'd forgotten that."

"You'd forgotten your name?"

"Jake calls me that. I never use it."

Luke paced up and down his side of the shadowed gazebo. Kyla dropped to the cold iron seat of a decorative chair, more confused than ever. "You have two names and you never use one of them?"

"It's complicated."

"This whole damn thing is complicated!"

His step drummed on the wooden floor until he stood before her. He crouched to sit on his heels, his tangy scent blending with the perfume of the garden. "My name . . . my legal name is Lucien Morainge."

"And Luke Hudson is your illegal name."

"My father wasn't married to my mother." Kyla swayed. If he'd wanted to hit her broadside, he'd succeeded. "When she found out she was pregnant, she also found out he was married. Despite the betrayal and heartbreak, she wanted her baby to 'have a name.' His name. Morainge. For when I was older, she said, so I'd know he had cared. He acknowledged paternity on my birth certificate . . . to put an end to her hounding, I imagine. She meant well, but our having different names only magnified the fact that I was illegitimate. I first heard the word 'bastard' in relation to me when I was in the first grade—"

Kyla sucked in a painful breath. Her hands flew to her mouth as if to shove back that vile name she'd uttered earlier. "Oh, Luke . . . I didn't . . . I'm . . ."

Smiling, he pulled her hands away from her face, replacing them in her lap and covering them with his own. "I know you didn't mean it that way."

"I still hate myself for saying it." His forgiveness was a warm gaze and a reassuring press on her hands.

"When I was eight, my mother married Mike Hudson. He loved me as much as he adored her. I thought it was over; I had a father. But it didn't stop the slurs. It didn't bring me friends. And it didn't make me his son. So Mike jumped on the legal tread-mill that would let him adopt me." Luke glanced away and Kyla saw the child's pain in his eyes, met the dejected little boy Beth Gainer had described. "I practiced my new name. I planned what I'd wear to court. Then the lawyer called. My birth father . . . they needed his permission. He had to relinquish rights to me first. My future rested with a man who, in nine years, never once bothered to see me—not even out of curiosity. And he refused to sign."

"Why, Luke?"

His broad shoulders rose and fell. "Who really knows? He said he wanted the name Morainge to go on. I was his only son. He and his wife had never had kids. So the adoption didn't take place. No one in the mountains knew about me; we were just another family—the Hudson family. The three of us let it happen. It was a small deception. The first time someone introduced me as Luke Hudson, I didn't correct them. Who was I hurting? In the mountains I was Mike Hudson's boy, not Tom Morainge's bastard. So when Jake introduced me to you that way, I didn't even notice."

He traced the delicate veins in the hollow of her wrist with a gentle fingertip. His head was bent over her lap and Kyla lovingly combed his hair with her eyes.

"Any more questions?" he asked.

A hundred, Kyla thought. A thousand. But the answers wouldn't make any difference.

"I watched you tonight," he muttered. "Do you know you touch people? When you talk to people, you reach for their hands, rest your fingers on their sleeves." His wounded eyes hurt her. "You've never touched me first, Kyla. You've never reached out to me."

Not until he mentioned it had she realized that she needed to touch people when she talked to them. It seemed necessary, part of the connecting. "Are you jealous?" she asked incredulously.

"No," he whispered. "I know who you love." Kyla's heart tumbled into her stomach. "But you didn't trust me. Not even after you knew I loved you. Do you now?"

"Luke, we're competitors. I *can't* trust you now." It broke her heart to say it. "When I first saw you tonight and Andrew told me you were Lucien Morainge, I tried to convince myself the man I loved had a double, that this couldn't be happening. But it *was* happening . . . it *is* happening. The worst is true, Luke. Too painfully true."

He released her hands with a sigh and stood up. Jamming his hands in his pockets, he began backing away. Kyla tipped her head back to look at him, and something in his eyes chilled her. "We haven't gotten to the worst of it, Kyla. That's next, I'm afraid."

Her mouth went dry. Foreboding raised the fine hairs on her arms. "What is the worst?" she whispered.

"It's my job to weaken CompuMart in the marketplace. In short, to destroy your company's financial base and buy it out."

Kyla sat still as stone, staring up at his face. Once again joy had disintegrated and the dream dissolved. He wasn't just the competition. He was the enemy.

Eight

He caught her as she flew out of the gazebo. She was spun around and hauled up to his chest by the powerful grip of his hands on her upper arms. Kyla didn't fight, didn't breathe. She just stared at him with growing panic.

"Why? Why CompuMart? Go after someone else. Heaven knows there are hundreds of us little guys for Quantum to gobble up." She wouldn't let herself plead, although she wanted to cry: *Don't take it from me. I've worked five years for this. This is mine!*

"Come back and sit down, tenderfoot."

"No!" That name, that damned pet name, infuriated her. "Don't call me that. I am *not* a tenderfoot. Not here, Luke. This is my territory . . . it's what I do best. I am no greenhorn. Forget the bumbling fool you met in the mountains."

His punishing clamp on her slim arms eased enough for feeling to return. They were both silent, gazing across the inches that separated their faces, their mouths, their mingling breaths. He didn't say it. He didn't have to—she read it in his eyes. She might not be a tenderfoot here, but it was his turf. He was . . . What had he called himself? A knowledgeable native. Yes, he was still the master.

"Why us, Luke?"

Turning her, he tucked her under his arm. "Us, CompuMart? Or us, you and me?"

Kyla wrapped her arm around his waist as he walked her toward the balcony steps. It was the most natural thing in the world for her to do, lean on his strength, at least until she got her bearings. "Both." She sighed. "But let's start with CompuMart."

"Because the Quantum board of directors wants it. And it's my job to give 'em what they want."

"We've never won awards. We don't gross in the billions. There's nothing to distinguish us from the countless other companies doing what we do." It wasn't like her to discount CompuMart's reputation. But, like the vestal virgin to the rake, she cried: *You don't want me. I'm unattractive.* "Who laid us at their feet?"

"I refuse to answer on the grounds . . . Ah, love." With his free hand he vigorously rubbed his forehead.

How many more blows did this day have in store for her? "So give them someone else. Make them want another company."

"Too late. The research, the man-hours . . ."

They walked the veranda, their voices automatically dropping to low murmurs as they passed the guest rooms. At her door, Kyla turned, pressing her back to the glass panes. "Tell me why, Luke."

"Hi-Life."

She blinked, her mind racing. Working. "That's my client. I signed them up."

"Is that so? You *are* good. Did a phenomenal job with them. In fact, you've got them sewn up so tight, the only way for me to acquire their business is to go after CompuMart."

"I don't understand." Kyla mentally pulled the Hi-Life file. A stereo/radio/tape-deck supplier. San

Diego-based, nine branches in and around the area. Small but regular orders. Resisted new programs. No computers beyond the basic home type. "It's a nice account, but that's it . . . a nice account. We could survive without them, and it sure as hell wouldn't pay Quantum's monthly phone bill."

"Why the six-year wrap-up?"

"It's a test market. My own." His eyes were curious; she'd intrigued him. "Their stores are well spaced throughout San Diego, a good cross section of a manageable population. L.A. would have been too big. The average Hi-Life customer is a teenager from a middle-income home with a pretty solid education. Tomorrow's customer. I wanted to see if familiarity with a product would affect their future buying patterns. So we stock the Hi-Life stores with basic computers and lots of games to play on them."

"Interesting. What sort of statistics are you looking for?"

"We aren't sure. A market team is putting together the analysis data. That's why I've got them tied up for six years. We won't even begin getting results for two, maybe three years. I wanted to know we'd still be in their stores when the teens of today were in college before I justified what it would cost to monitor the test."

"You think the college student will be the next key market."

"I think we've wandered very far from the subject at hand." Pulling her arms across her chest, she cupped her elbows in her hands. "Quantum has a superior research department, so I doubt it's my measly little survey you guys want."

He shook his head, watching her closely. "Hi-Life is negotiating to acquire National Office Supplies."

She'd never heard of them. "And?"

"And, my contact reports it's as good as done."

"And?" She drew the word out, sensing the gathering thunderclap.

He gave her a long look. "And, NOS is a national chain handling everything for the office, from a Chippendale desk to a paper clip. Everything but computers. After acquisition, NOS will service business offices the way Hi-Life services teenagers. One-stop shopping, from plants to peripherals, carpets to computers. In all one-hundred and eighty-two outlets."

A fortune! Numbers so staggering Kyla could barely calculate them. And it was her account! If it went through, it would *make* her in the industry. The packaging would be a dream . . . if she still had them to package. "You'd do that to me?"

"I have to."

"I have to stop you."

He nodded, understanding. "You have to try." His eyes pleaded for equal understanding, something she couldn't possibly grant. "I love you." He took her shoulders and shook her, as if to make the words register. "I love you, Kyla. But that has nothing to do with Quantum or CompuMart."

Then his mouth covered hers, bruising and harsh. And she knew he was trying to blot the ruthless vision of him from her mind. With open hands she pushed against his chest, but with her lips she clung to him. Heaven and hell, she thought restlessly. The wrong man was so right for her. "No, Luke. We can't."

"Like hell we can't." His hands stroked her sides from ribs to hips. His lips nibbled at her mouth. His scent became the air she breathed. "I've missed you, love."

Not half as much, she thought. *Not a quarter.* He caressed the gentle dip of spine at her waist as his tongue slipped sweetly past her lips, assuaging that which he'd just tormented. She never felt him twist the knob pressed to her back, but followed the door's path over the threshold, bringing Luke with her.

He shut it softly, the click of the latch jolting Kyla to her senses. "You can't stay, Luke."

"I can't leave, love."

Kyla *felt* Andrew's presence on the other side of the wall she was plastered to. If he ever found out . . . Last week she honestly hadn't known who Luke was. She had no such excuse now. "Luke, this is wrong. We're breaking the most basic rule of business. This is consorting. And you're the enemy. If my boss or your board found out, we'd both be ruined." Yet there was something wildly erotic in feasting on forbidden fruits, she admitted.

"I've got news for you, love. This is *not* what they don't want us to do. Talking on a park bench would probably get both of us canned—"

"No one will believe we aren't—"

"Shh." His fingers covered her lips. "Don't talk. Let the silence be our loyalty. Let my body share secrets with you."

All of her senses rushed to her lips, squeezing the pleasure from his touch.

"Hmm?" he murmured.

She nodded, her gaze liquid and blurring. Her flesh wanting and ready.

An abrasive brush preceded the lift of his fingers from her mouth. Kyla dragged her tongue over her lips, finding the taste of him there.

He pinched the streamer of white ribbon resting on her shoulder, and slowly drew it down. The bow fell apart, releasing a curtain of wild hair. Pressing his palms to the wall at either side of her, he gazed down, his eyes cataloging her features. Rigid arms held him away, depriving her breasts of the hard crush of his chest. Crackling tension electrified the moonlit space between them.

"Touch me, Kyla," he murmured, his eyes begging her response. "Touch me first. I want . . . *need* you to reach out and touch me."

His need was important to her. All the giving to this point had been on his part. All the strength. All the expertise. But now she saw that the hand extended had to be hers. She wanted to heal him of all the touches denied in his lifetime.

Kyla began to move her hands, lighting on the knot of his tie, when suddenly she remembered how he had once carried her fingers over his face. How he had shuddered with the pleasure of it. So she lifted her hands and smoothed his temples, stroked his brow, then brushed the forest of gold lashes that fell over his glazed eyes.

Dragging her thumb across his lips, she separated them, licking moisture onto her own. She curved her palm to his throat and felt the blood hammer through his veins.

"So hard. Your pulse is pounding."

"More than my pulse, love."

Tie and shirt fell open under her fingers. No longer gentle, her hands tore over hard muscle, crisp hair, satin belly. She fell to his sinewed strength, murmuring for his mouth as she finished stripping him with frantic shoves at fabric. Their kisses were greedy and quick, not always accurate, lips falling on chin or jaw as Luke shifted to assist her in removing his shoes and socks.

Naked at last, he ravaged her mouth with his tongue. His hands tunneled through her hair, urgently rushed over throat and shoulders, carried the spaghetti straps of her nightgown along with her robe down her arms. Precariously perched on her breasts, the soft cloth began slipping. She released a long sigh, the collapse of her chest dropping all covering to her waist.

Luke searched the folds to find the sash and untie it. Silk and lace fell with a whisper. He caught her in his arms, holding her at the hips and lifting her high. Kyla clutched handfuls of hair, trying to hold onto her sanity, as Luke tongued her nipples. The storm of passion began whipping through her.

"Oh, Luke . . . I missed you so much."

He laid her across the bed, her hair pouring over

the mattress edge, her arms open. Her nails curled to her palms as Luke celebrated her flesh with his hot, greedy mouth. He stirred and blessed it. He woke and thrilled it. His touch taught her how fragile she was to him—not the delicacy of bone, but the dearness of heart.

When passion at last fused them into one being, Kyla clung to Luke as if she'd never let him go. Then, as she fought her way back to air from the small drowning, her arms relaxed, falling heavily away, and she knew she would not hold him again for a long time . . . would not make love with him at night while she fought him by day.

Luke lazily skimmed her flesh under the sheets they had crawled between. Through passion-fogged eyes Kyla gazed at him. Tangled gold hair graced the crisp white pillowcase; his hard shoulders mocked the sheet's lacy border.

With a groan he eased out of bed. Kyla rolled to her stomach, hugging the pillow under her chin as she watched the fluid movements of his body as he dressed. When he pulled on tight briefs, Kyla looked surprised. "Because you're in the city?"

"Because I'm in a wool suit. Very scratchy stuff."

"Luke?"

"Mmm."

"What territories did you overstep on this Opticillusion thing?"

His smile grew empty. This was precisely the reason competitors couldn't, shouldn't, and if they were smart, *didn't* have affairs with each other, and she knew it. The temptation to ask one small question was always there.

"Just tell me if we're the only ones."

"You're the only ones."

A sad whisper accompanied the soft rustle of his clothes. *Good-bye*, it said, *I'm leaving now.*

"I have a meeting with the Visionary people at eight." Kyla watched his reaction, noting a hesitation in the fingers buttoning his shirt.

"Jacket?" He glanced around the dim room.

"In the gazebo."

"You be careful, Kyla. Don't take on more than you can handle."

"Mmm. Funny, that was my first thought when I met you."

Dressed like a back-alley lover, with socks in his pockets and tie loosely draped around his shoulders, he sat on the edge of the bed. His eyes leisurely toured her nakedness above the sheets twisted at her waist.

"Do you remember the rules of survival in the mountains?" He waited for her nod of assent. "They apply here too. Keep that in mind, you'll do okay."

Finding it absurd to conduct a business discussion naked, Kyla drew the covers up to her chin. He smiled at her after-the-fact modesty and stood.

"I'm going after your commitment, Luke. What with the Hi-Life information—"

"Don't count your mountains before you climb them, tenderfoot." He was walking away, so he didn't see the angry press of her lips at the infuriating endearment. "First, no bank in the world is going to finance your initial delivery on a third-hand rumor, no matter how 'in the bag' it is. Second, where will you tell them you heard it? From me? The man you're planning to beat out of the deal? While you were in bed with me?"

"I can't do nothing, Luke." She sat up, forgetting to bring the covers with her. Luke's slow, seductive smile and the smoldering gaze sent Kyla's eyes to the mirror on the opposite wall. In the uncertain light, she was a pale reflection against creamy sheets, counterpointed by the large dark eyes framed in wild, fiery hair. Her nipples had the same thoroughly kissed pout as her mouth.

"Oh, Lord, Luke, what are we going to do?"

The sorrow etching her eyes told him exactly what she referred to. "We're going to battle it out, love." Opening the door, he stepped out and smiled at her over his shoulder. "I expect it will be a good fight, Kyla. You're a pro, a worthy opponent."

And then he was gone. The metallic click of the door shutting echoed like the report of a gun in the stillness. As she dragged her eyes from the door, her gaze caught a wink of gold in the blue carpet. One of his cuff links had fallen out of his pocket. Sinew and sweat, and French cuffs too, she noted regretfully.

The clock read four in the morning. She got out of bed and went to the heap of nightgown and robe, separating them and drawing on the robe over her nakedness. Then she picked up the brushed-gold cuff link and slipped it into her pocket. *Survival rule number one: Take no less than you can carry and no more than you need.* Pulling a sheet of hotel stationery from the dresser drawer, Kyla turned on the lamp at the small writing table and went to work.

At six-fifteen she showered. At six-thirty she dialed Vince Hawthorne's room.

"Uh-mph . . ." he grumbled, half-asleep.

"Vince? It's Kyla. Can I stop by your room in about fifteen minutes? I've got some numbers I need to go over with you."

"Mmm . . ." She took the mutter for an affirmative.

It was closer to half an hour before she actually knocked on his door. And bless Vince, room service was three steps behind her with two pots of coffee.

Kyla walked into the hotel coffee shop, as prepared to save CompuMart as she'd ever be. Her slim white skirt coupled with four inch heels was meant to give the illusion of height to her petite stature. The lively apple-green cowl-neck sweater gave her the appearance of energy that her body was drained of.

Bob Christman waved from a table and introduced her to the man and woman already seated. Her exhausted brain promptly forgot their last names and for the rest of the meeting she addressed them as Linda and Greg. Kyla described her proposal, sensing a willingness on their part to arrive at a mutually agreeable compromise. Christman took a back seat in the discussion and Kyla suspected Visionary was not thrilled with how he had handled things so far.

Linda glanced over her notes, wiping crumbs of a prune Danish from her fingers. "So what you're asking for, Kyla, is limited exclusivity."

Kyla preferred not to use those words, although essentially that was the case. "What I'm asking for is first delivery, with thirty percent of my commitment in the first quarter and a commitment *in writing* that no other distributor in the Los Angeles/San Diego region take delivery on Opticillusion until we've had it in hand for ninety days." Vince had gone over the numbers with her, wincing at the resultant financial risk but agreeing with Kyla that they could swing it. "In return, we'll up our take to a million-three."

Gold-flecked eyes studied Kyla from across the table. It's still limited exclusivity, the look said. Linda then sat back and lit a long, thin cigarette, calculating the profits to Visionary Tech. They could increase their order from CompuMart by three hundred thousand dollars and still keep Quantum's million-dollar order.

"Do you see anything in this that botches the deal with Morainge?" Linda asked Bob.

"No problem," he said. Kyla released her held breath in a slow, unnoticeable stream. *Reprieved.*

"Will you accept an addendum to the contract?" Greg asked. "Or do we draw up a new one?"

Kyla wanted it on paper, and she wanted it on paper today, before Luke got wind of it. "An addendum will be fine. As soon as I sign it, I'm on my way back to L.A."

Two hours later Kyla boarded the air shuttle to Los Angeles. She'd been awake for nearly twenty-eight hours. By the time she walked into her condo, it had been closer to thirty-two. Hours packed with a year's worth of shocks to her system. She took the phone off the hook, pulled the clothes off her body, and fell naked between the sheets.

Nine

*This company needs more women in manage-
ment,* Kyla thought, scanning the disparate male-to-
female ratio of the group gathered in her office. She
sat behind her Plexiglas-topped desk, silent but
observant, as Vince Hawthorne held court, reviewing
Opticillusion data for the assembled managers, setting up hands-on demonstration times, and stressing the importance of the first ninety days in three
words: sell, sell sell. There were six men to one woman
in the note-taking bunch. Kyla didn't count herself or
her secretary, Martha Kronk.

Presently Martha teetered on a stepladder, taking
advantage of the informal work session to put down
her steno pad and hang a couple of paintings that
had just arrived. Two absent lithographs that had
belonged to Frank Hooper had left unsightly bleached
rectangles, revealing once-white walls. The new color-
splashed canvases, while costing Kyla money, at least
saved her the inconvenience of trying to work around
painters. They also livened the sterile chrome-and-
glass decor of the vice-president's domain, which,

like the rest of the executive offices, had about as much warmth as the inside of a computer.

When her phone rang, Kyla signaled Martha not to bother climbing down, she'd get it herself. "Kyla Trent," she informed the caller.

" 'Morning, love." His deep voice stroked her senses so that she actually shuddered in response. Kyla hazarded a guilty glance at the faces in the room before realizing how paranoid that was. They couldn't know she was talking to Lucien Morainge.

"Good morning," she responded levelly. "What can I do for you?"

She heard his soft chuckle, pictured the radiance bathing his face when he laughed. She gripped the receiver a little tighter, holding his voice in lieu of him. "Whatever you'd like, love, Surf's up today. How about joining me for a romp in the ocean? I know of this secluded beach where we could—"

"I have a full schedule, I'm afraid." She rotated her ice-blue swivel chair to face the window, feeling conspicuously transparent to those in the room. He sounds all right, she thought in relief. She'd been jumpy as a cat ever since putting her phone back on the hook at midnight Saturday. It had been wrong to leave San Francisco without seeing him, telling him. But it was the adversary she'd left at the time. After sleep and a light meal, she'd wondered how the lover would take it.

"A coffee break in the back seat of my car?"

"You've caught me at an inconvenient time."

"You're not alone. In that case, I'll settle for lunch."

"I'm sorry, that isn't possible." Kyla gazed at the distant mountains outside her windows, a hazy purple silhouette beyond the city, and wished she were back there with Luke. That the weekend had never happened. That the future could be as simple and joyful as she had thought it would be when she'd left him at the cabin.

"I'll see you at one o'clock, love. And I hope to hell your office door doesn't have a lock on it."

He hung up. Lord, he can't come here! she thought wildly. Andrew, Vince, half the people in the place knew him!

This is dumb, Kyla, she told herself. Dumb, dumb, dumb. She didn't even know what kind of car he drove. She paced the sidewalk in front of Compu-Mart, glancing up and down the boulevard. The only way she could think of to prevent Luke from breezing into her office, stirring up every sort of speculation—one bound to be correct—was to waylay him on the street. Perspiration rolled down her sides under her cinnamon silk dress. The sharp sun and baking pavement were turning her cream linen jacket to soggy tissue.

Susie Barrett exited CompuMart's front door as Kyla leaned on a corner lamppost where she could watch the intersection.

"Hey, Kyla," she called. "Wanna join me for lunch?" Susie had the effervescence of a champagne bubble, constantly celebrating life. If there were a distinction between a receptionist and a vice-president, Susie couldn't have cared less.

"Thanks, no. I'm waiting for someone."

Surprise widened Susie's eyes. "Out here? Kyla, guess what?" Her secretive whisper nearly stopped Kyla's heart. Had Luke given his name to Susie when he'd called? Did the girl suspect? "You're the veep now. That's what your waiting room is for . . . for waiting in."

"Oh." Kyla drew a relieved breath. Go to lunch, Susie! she wanted to scream. It was almost one o'clock. "This has to be a fast bite with a client. I didn't want him to waste time parking just to come in for me."

And then Kyla saw him at the end of the block,

walking head and shoulders above the lunch crowd. A cab pulled up at the corner and discharged a passenger. Panicked, Kyla grabbed the open door and Susie's elbow, dumping the girl in the cab's back seat. "What luck, Susie."

"But, Kyla . . . wait, Kyla . . ."

"Have a nice lunch." Kyla slammed the door and waved.

"But, Kyla . . ." Susie leaned out the window as the cab pulled away. "I'm just going up the street to McDonald's."

Very dumb, Kyla, she thought. He doesn't just make you act like an adolescent, but like an idiot as well. Then she turned on her heel and rushed toward Luke before anyone else from CompuMart could leave the building. Heaven only knew what ridiculous thing she might do next.

When he saw her hurrying in his direction, his face lit up. Kyla's feet slowed as her heart began to race, unprepared for his striking good looks, weakened by the caress of his eyes. She still wasn't used to seeing him in tailored suits with elegant airs, even though he wore both superbly. When he captured her fingertips and used them to walk her up to his chest, Kyla became aware of the crowd bumping around them, of how besotted she must look. Drawing her hands out of his, she stepped away. "Don't."

"Don't what?"

"Don't do anything that . . . that makes it look like we're together." She moved on, trying to keep some distance by staying ahead of him. But no matter how fast she sprinted, Luke remained at her side, lengthening his stride without once breaking out of an easy walk. She flew into a fast-food place, saw three salesmen from CompuMart sitting at the counter, and flew out again.

Halfway down the next block, Luke grabbed her elbow and pulled her through a restaurant doorway. "This should be perfect," he said. "Dim lighting, private booths, and a bar. I have a feeling I'm going to need a stiff drink to get through this."

After the bright light outside, Kyla had to squint through the restaurant's discreet gloom. When she didn't see anyone she knew, her shoulders relaxed. Luke asked for a booth in the back. His request was simply and quietly stated, but Kyla detected the faint sarcasm lost on the maître d'.

When they were seated, she buried her face behind the marquee-size menu, gulping three deep breaths to force down her rising temper. Luke plucked the green leather folder from her fingers. "Give the man your order."

"Coffee and the French onion soup," she told the waiter, poised with his pen and pad.

"Scotch and water," Luke said. "Make her coffee a sweet vermouth on the rocks. And we'll both have the T-bone, cottage fries, and tossed salad with house dressing."

"Look—" Kyla began.

"You're strung tight as a bow," Luke interrupted as the waiter moved away. "If I don't feed you, you're liable to eat the tablecloth."

"Luke," she began again. "I can't stay that long. I really do have a full afternoon and we really should not see each other." He watched her, his head tilted, his mouth curving—why, she amused him! "Don't you dare look at me like that!"

"Like what?"

"As if I'm a . . . a naive tenderfoot looking for scorpions in my sleeping bag."

"You don't think you're overreacting to a simple lunch invitation?" He loosened his tie, slipped the first two buttons on his shirt open, and spread his arms over the back of the banquette. But he wasn't relaxed, Kyla decided, noticing the flex and hold of muscle beneath his suit, fractionally shifting the folds of material. He had adopted the appearance of a casual man, but he was prepared to take the first blow.

"No. Obviously you do. My receptionist Susie Barrett no doubt will think I overreacted to *her* lunch invitation." Their waiter returned, setting the Scotch in front of Luke, a coffee in front of Kyla, and the vermouth in the center of the table.

Luke smiled. "You can please all of the people some of the time. Now, tell me what you did with Susie."

"I put her in a cab. She didn't want a cab, but I didn't let a little thing like that stop me." Kyla closed her eyes and shook her head. "Susie must weigh a hundred and thirty pounds. She's at least seven inches taller than I am and I *bodily* put her in a cab because I was afraid she'd see you."

Kyla took a steadying breath and laced her fingers together on the snowy tablecloth. Wariness edged the jade eyes gazing across the table at her. *This is how it will always be between us,* she thought. *This is why it won't work.* There could be moments when he'd be her lover, but he would always be her adversary.

"Did you take your phone off the hook Saturday just to avoid my call?"

"No. Honest, Luke, I didn't. I sleep lightly and didn't want it to wake me. I never did go to bed Friday night."

"Wrong. You may not have slept. But I distinctly remember you in bed."

Her thoughts, arranged in some semblance of order, scattered like a dropped box of straight pins. She felt the resultant prickles all the way to her toes as she too remembered . . . the torrid loving on lacy sheets . . . the hard flesh covering soft.

"And Sunday? Why didn't you answer?"

"I was with my brother Steve and his family in La Jolla."

"You didn't tell me you had a brother in California."

Her thick lashes lowered as she smiled wryly. "There were a lot of subjects we neglected to discuss, don't you think?"

"Tell me about him."

He was changing subjects on her again. He had done it at their first dinner together when he'd sensed she needed the time to gather her wits. "Steve is a year older than I am, so I'm closer to him than my other two brothers. He and his wife, Barb, and their three girls have a beach house in La Jolla and he runs a very successful chain of sporting-goods stores. He's the reason that, when I left Chicago, I came to California. He offered a shoulder to lean on and free room and board while I got on my feet."

When she finished, he was watching her intently. "Then you didn't avoid my calls this weekend. And you aren't planning to in the future."

She dropped her eyes to focus on the ice floating in the untouched glass of vermouth. "We are competing rivals, Luke. Career enemies. Do you know what they call a woman who sleeps with a man who shares her profession? I do." She sipped her coffee, feeling his emotions coil and begin winding around her. "See, I've been here before. I've heard the malicious innuendos, I've seen the leers."

"Fullerton."

"Right. Only he wasn't the competition. He was my boss." In an unemotional voice Kyla gave him all the gory details, sparing none. She told him everything, stressing how suddenly the accomplishments so proudly listed on her résumé were discounted as having been bartered for in a bedroom, rather than bargained for in a boardroom.

"He sounds like a real son of a bitch," Luke pronounced succinctly.

Kyla sighed. "A son of a bitch who came out smelling like a rose. Not so for me," she finished bitterly, then locked her enormous dark eyes on him. "No, Luke."

"No? What are you saying 'no' to, Kyla?" The voice was dangerously soft.

"Everything. No lunches, dinners, or coffee breaks. No phone calls. No dates. No talking." He covered her folded hands with his own and squeezed. "No touching."

"Do you love me, Kyla?"

"Luke—"

"Do you love me?"

"You know I do. And that—"

"Is all that matters."

Kyla found she had no appetite for the feast laid before her and pushed her plate away to draw restless patterns on the padded tablecloth with one fingernail. "If you acquire CompuMart," she said, "people will say I lost it because my hands were busy holding something else. If I manage to keep it, they'll never say it was because of my *professional* abilities. Win or lose, you'll look just fine. The mythical male fraternity will sympathize, pat you on the back, poke you in the ribs, say, 'Who could resist, old man? A broad lies down at your feet, you gotta do what you gotta do.'"

"Stop that and—"

"No, you stop!" Kyla managed to put a tremendous amount of force into those few words without raising her voice. "And think back to last Friday. What was the first thing you thought when you saw me at the Visionary dinner? Didn't you assume I'd gotten wind of your plans to acquire CompuMart? That I'd slept with you because of it?"

"That was the confusion of the man who loves you." But spiteful names and undeserved scorn were things Luke had painful firsthand knowledge of, she remembered. Kyla saw compassionate understanding enter his eyes—and she saw the determination fight it. "So we're careful. No one will know."

"I'll know." Kyla shook her head against his unspoken plea. "It's unethical. And I'll know."

"How long before you'll see me again?" He downed his drink and signaled for another.

"How long before you stop trying to undermine my company?"

He twirled his empty glass on the table, his mouth twisting up on one side. "Hmm. I'd thought it would be a quick and painless job, but I've run into an unexpectedly astute opponent. That ninety-day jump with Visionary hurt me, Kyla."

She raised a cool brow and smiled. "No one quite as indignant as the biter bit."

"One point for your side. You're a good strategist. Unfortunately, it's going to drag the battle out."

"That's how long."

"Kyla, in all honesty, would you want me to back away from my responsibility to Quantum for the sole reason that I loved you?"

"No." That would have been the ultimate in mixing the personal and professional life, the very thing Kyla found abhorrent. "No more than you'd want me to back off from fighting you."

"Feel free to back off." She narrowed her eyes on him. "I like to win, love. I'm not real fussy how I do it."

"Or whom you destory to do it?"

"Ah, love, I'd never hurt you. In fact, I'll help you whenever I can."

Kyla glared furiously at him. "I don't need your help, dammit. I don't want your help."

When she left the restaurant, she did so without having eaten, and alone. Halfway across the dining room she heard his voice, unsure whether he was speaking to her or to himself: "You'll be seeing me, love."

Four days later Kyla learned of Luke's counter-stroke to her limited exclusivity.

"Problems, Kyla," Vince Hawthorne said, sticking his head in her door. "You want it now or in the morning?"

Kyla closed the file on her desk. "Let's have it now."

"Getting some fallout on the Opticillusion clients." He rolled his unlit cigar from left to right in his mouth. Kyla couldn't stomach the smell of cigar smoke in her office, and Vince obliged her by crushing his ash out before meeting with her. "Some of them were pretty committed."

"Give any reasons?"

"Sure they do." He grunted in disgust. "Quantum's offering an extended ninety-day warranty. So they're willing to wait till the first of the year."

"Oh, boy." Kyla sighed. There was nothing she could do against that kind of thrust, except hope they didn't bleed too badly. Not only did CompuMart lack the necessary technicians to service that many units, they lacked the funds to hire them. She smiled wryly, thinking: *You got me, Luke, measure for measure; ninety days for ninety days. Two points for your side.*

"Tell the sales force to stay on top of it. Stress our support. Go easy on the hard sell. Visionary's already primed them to want it, let's not turn anyone off by being pushy."

"We can always hope for a back order from Visionary, buy us another month or two, make Quantum that much less inviting."

"Lord, Vince, don't even *think* that word. We need Opticillusion delivered on time."

"Why? Whether it comes next month or the one after, Quantum doesn't get it until three months *after* we have it. There's a limit to how long people will wait."

"There's also a limit to how much people will take. And we have to keep these people happy. We supply retailers. For every one of our customers we disappoint, he disappoints twenty. How would you feel toward a supplier who didn't supply, and left you with twenty angry customers to handle? We'll lose some of them for the sheer vengeance of it . . . even if they do have to wait longer to get it from Lu— Quantum."

"Well, you don't know people like they've got back in the Valley. Kyla, you know why manufacturers always hold these seminars in hotels? Why you only meet the boys in the brown suits and horn-rimmed glasses? Because they don't want you to stumble on the inventors at the plant. A crazier bunch you never did see. Bug-eyed geniuses playing with memory chips so small I couldn't fit my laundry list on it. They make up electronic war games in their spare time!" Kyla bit her lower lip to keep from laughing at Vince's confounded expression. "They don't care about contracts, deadlines, or bank loans. If some damn blip isn't to their liking, they'll pull the line until it is."

"Christman was quite positive Opticillusion would roll off on time."

"Opticillusion is already six months over its target date. And we're still thirty days from the rescheduled debut."

Kyla leaned back, rocking her desk chair. "I can always count on you to depress me, Vince."

"Just doing my job." He grinned around the mashed stub in his mouth. "Anything else I can do for you while I'm here?"

"Yes. You can ask Bill Danvers to stop comparing a computer to a brain for the intimidated client. The metaphor is hardly enlightening. Who do you know outside of psychiatrists and neurologists with the smallest inkling of how a brain works? Suggest he compare it to a filing system. Everybody understands a filing system."

"Is that so?" Martha came in, carrying a tray of fresh coffee. "I'd like to put that theory to the test."

"I'll talk to him," Vince said, taking a brimming mug of coffee from Martha's tray before she could whisk it out of his reach. "He's just inflating himself by stuffing other people with his college education."

Vince left and Martha offered a few choice words about cigar smoke, overweight, and crude manners.

"Martha, bring me this week's invoices, then you can go home."

"And leave you here alone in this building? Have you see the night cleaning crew?" Martha's naturally pinched face drew tighter with disgust. "Looks like they all escaped from Alcatraz. I'll stay as long as you do."

Kyla chuckled. "My mother would appreciate knowing I have you."

Martha stopped on the threshold and grinned lecherously over her shoulder. "And maybe one of them will attack me in a deserted hallway." Then she left to collect the invoices Kyla had requested. Taking a mug of coffee, Kyla walked to the window to stare out the slats of her window blinds. There he was. Sitting on the park bench across the street, reading the evening paper. Every night for the last four. And every luncheon appointment found him across the room in the same restaurant. She was seeing Luke, all right— every time she turned around.

"Does it make you happy, Mr. Morainge, watching me work till midnight, trying to thwart what you do in an average day?" She sighed and adjusted the blinds to an angle that wouldn't allow incriminating light to seep out.

"Who were you talking to?" Martha asked, setting a folder that was frighteningly slim on Kyla's desk.

"My shadow, Martha. Just my shadow."

"A Mr. Luke Hudson is on the phone," Martha called through the intercom. "He won't say what it's about. Seems pretty sure you'll take the call, though."

"Yes, I'll take it." Kyla punched the flashing

phone button, grateful he hadn't used the name Morainge.

"Good morning, love."

"Luke, you have to stop following me. It . . . it unnerves me."

"Why? I'm always dressed. I don't—"

"Please, Luke. Stop."

"All right, love," he conceded.

"Was there something about Opticillusion you wanted to discuss?"

"No. I was sitting here remembering the waterfall we visited in the mountains. And I wanted to talk to you."

"The waterfall?" Kyla stirred uneasily in her chair. It was not one of her favorite memories. "And laughing at me for thinking the roar of the waterfall was thunder?"

"Don't make that mistake now, love. Too often things are not what they seem."

"Okay." Kyla took the phone away from her ear and frowned at it. What a strange conversation for two adversaries to have, she thought.

"The wrong step, it could all come tumbling down. 'Bye, love."

Kyla hung up, her forehead creased in concern. On the surface, it appeared to be an innocent, unconventional phone call, but she wondered what really was behind it.

"Does Andrew know that Quantum's out to get us?"

Chuck Myers nearly knocked Kyla off her chair with his complacent question. His back was to her, so he didn't see her fingers curl and tighten on her chair.

"Why do you think that, Chuck?" He had taken her promotion well. Oh, he would have preferred to be sitting on Kyla's side of the desk instead of dropping into the chair across from her. But he'd admitted to her after the announcement that he'd expected all along she'd be the one named. Brad Upton had not taken it quite as charitably, avoiding any room occupied by Kyla these last two weeks. She'd have to deal with him, and soon. For now, Chuck Myers had her full attention.

"They danced all over the Opticillusion deal. Now I've had three reports from retailers that Quantum's going to discount their whole inventory the first of the month."

Damn, he was shooting at them with both barrels. "Rumors."

"Everyone wants to know if we'll cut. What's our answer?"

"How dependable are the customers reporting this?"

"I trust them. And three in one day, Kyla. Pretty strong evidence it's gonna happen. Quantum's dumping . . . and we'll be buried in our own stock if we don't follow suit. If it were me I'd be on the phone this minute taking five percent off everything we've got."

Well, it isn't you, Kyla wanted to snap. "We're at a minimum profit margin now."

"You're the boss lady, but keep in mind that the bank is going to be taking a close look at our month-end statement before they advance the check on the initial delivery of Opticillusion. You'll need some healthy numbers there. And right now, no one is buying, afraid we're going to be forced to cut in the next few weeks."

"Let me think about it, Chuck."

He stood up to leave. "Well, think fast. Quantum's cut down half a dozen distribution firms in the last two years and my gut instincts say we're next. It'll be a damn miracle if we can beat Morainge without knocking ourselves out."

A miracle.

The wrong step, it could all come tumbling down, love.

How very interesting, Kyla thought. She remembered the climb up the boulders to the waterfall she had called a miracle . . . and Luke's instructions. *Test your foothold before putting your weight down.*

"Martha, get me Daniel Prost on the phone, please." When the buzzer signaled her call was ready, Kyla answered in her friendliest voice. "Dan, I've been looking over your latest order. I don't think you want that particular computer line."

"Ah, the lovely lady wants to sell me a better product, mmm? And maybe more expensive?" Easy humor gentled the old man's thick accent.

"No, in fact I'm recommending you carry one compatible in every way for less money."

"You take pity on an old man?"

"A shrewd man like you, Daniel? Never."

"Ach, I miss you. This new man, Upton? I don't like. Take this. Sign here. In, out—no time for tea, no time for talk. I like my little Kyla back." He sighed dramatically. "But the little Kyla is a big lady now. So you tell me why I don't want this machine Upton says will run the world one day."

"It's very good, I won't deny that. And I'm pushing it for the retailer who offers servicing. But I'm not impressed with their quality control. They're so back-ordered, they're making the damn things in semis parked behind their plant. How good can a product be that comes out of a truck?"

"No! I don't want it. I made my oldest son in the back of a pickup and he never works. No computers made in trucks for me."

"You might be able to get the model I'm recommending cheaper from Quantum. We hear they've dropped their prices."

"I touch nothing from them. My son, he's not so bright, but he's my son, and they wipe him out." Kyla knew that, of course. Dan's son had owned one of the distribution companies that had fallen to Quantum recently.

"This is business, Dan. I think you should at least check it out."

"So I did already," he said. Kyla smiled to herself. She knew he'd go to the devil himself to get it for a buck less—son or no son. "They quote me same price. I don't know who start this about discounts. When I pull out my wallet, some old price."

"I'll have Upton call and adjust your order, Dan."

"Yah, and you come to dinner soon? My son, maybe if he have a wife like you, I don't worry what happens to him when I'm gone."

"Soon, Daniel."

Kyla assembled the sales force that afternoon. "We don't cut," she said, meeting the concerned scowls of both Chuck and Vince with complacence. "We don't cut," she repeated.

We draw on this round, Luke.

"Mr. Hudson on line one."

"Hello, love."

"Luke, no more flowers," Kyla begged. "I can't move around my office for all the vases. And they won't die!"

"Wildflowers have long lives. Much more stubborn than the delicate rose. I thought them appropriate for you."

Kyla glanced around the room at the tall, colorful snapdragons, the squat bowls of violets, the daisies in earthenware jugs. "No more, Luke."

"I've heard CompuMart is planning to hold prices. Is that a good idea?"

"It's a great idea. And you know it."

He laughed. Kyla had missed the low, rich sound almost as much as she missed his lips and his arms and his body beside her in bed. She knew a terrible frustration that she could have her integrity or Luke, but she couldn't have both. "If you've called to warn me of some new crisis and to propose how I can save myself, don't. I don't need you to save me, Luke."

"Not me, love. But about ten feet of rope should do it."

Rope. When had he used rope? To get her across the ravine. That had been about ten feet. Damn, she didn't want his help. But it was nearly impossible to ignore his phone call with the cryptic message. Rope. To tie the food up and secure it from predators. And if ever there was a predator! Okay, what did she have that Luke wanted? Clients. Hi-Life in particular. But they were wrapped, he'd already looked into that.

"Martha," Kyla called into her intercom. "Who was assigned to Hi-Life?"

"That would be Brad Upton. Most of your territory went to him."

"Thanks." It *would* have to be Upton, she thought. In this instance it was a good match. He didn't bother to update and neither did they. Kyla gambled that Luke wasn't going after a contract. No, he was going after a salesman, much the way Kyla had pirated Bowers away from Qauntum, bringing a healthy clientele with him. Brad was dissatisfied enough to leave CompuMart. Kyla simply had to ensure he left empty-handed.

"Martha," she called again. "Send me that new woman, the one I told you was ready to move into management."

"Patricia Potts."

"What are you trying to do, Kyla?" Brad Upton glared at Kyla across her desk, his face a livid purple.

"Would you care to sit down, Brad?"

"I don't need an assistant—"

"A trainee," Kyla corrected.

"That's crap and you know it. Patty Potts! Hell,

her name sounds like a doll you buy in the toy department. The clients laugh when they hear it."

Kyla made a temple of her fingers and stared over them at Brad. When she'd interviewed Patricia, Kyla had been thoroughly impressed. "You'll train her . . . show her the ropes. Then I'll assign her own territory."

"She's splitting *my* commission! *My* customers."

"Only on new clients. And only if she works with you to sign them."

Kyla was satisfied that Patricia understood her assignment—to court Brad's clients, pledge follow-up support, subtly impressing them with all that Brad didn't do for them.

"I don't have to sit still for this," Brad threatened.

Kyla shrugged and smiled. "My decisions have to be based on what's best for CompuMart, Brad."

Ten days later, he was gone. Triumphantly he announced to Kyla that he had been made an offer by Quantum that included better points than CompuMart gave him. Kyla had wished him luck. Andrew accepted her explanation that Brad had harbored hard feelings over the promotion. And Patricia kept the territory pretty much intact and in CompuMart's files.

"Mr. Hudson calling."

"Hello, love."

"Stop helping me, Luke." Kyla's voice was unnaturally tight, her control stretched thin by the strain. She was vaguely aware of standing at her desk and leaning over the phone.

"I'm not a vulture, tenderfoot."

"Just stop helping me!" Hearing the pet name snapped her control until she was screaming into the phone. "I don't need your help. I don't need anyone's help."

She slammed the phone down and saw Martha in the doorway in the same mortifying moment.

"In that case," Martha replied, "you won't mind if I skip out to the dentist this afternoon."

Unutterably exhausted, Kyla let herself in the front door of her condominium. It was the first time in over two weeks she'd arrived home with the sun still shining. It poured brightly through her wide windows. The yellow-and-green decor remained pale and delicate despite the harsh sunlight—a home designed not to overwhelm its owner. Splashing gaiety filtered in from the complex's community pool and Kyla decided that was precisely what she needed. A relaxing swim.

She was standing naked in her bedroom, bathing suit in hand, when the phone rang.

"Hello, love."

She groaned. "Luke." She pulled the sheet from her bed and wrapped it around her nakedness, feeling a vulnerability to Luke even through the phone. "Why did you call me? I told you—no more help."

There was a stretch of silence before his husky voice came over the line again and shivered in her veins. "I called to hear your voice, that's all. Because I miss you."

"Oh, Luke."

"Let me come over, Kyla."

"No."

"Then come here. I live in the hills, no one will see you—"

"No."

"Kyla—"

"I have to hang up now, Luke."

She swam until she thought she'd drop from exhaustion. And the next night, when he called, she swam again. Until it became a ritual. Every night. They talked on the phone, business was never mentioned, and then she swam her frustrations out in the pool long after the janitor had turned off the underwater lights.

Ten

"I don't care which of them you talk to, Kyla," Andrew said. "Susie or Bill. But talk to one of them."

Kyla pleated the material of her embroidered peasant skirt with her fingers, trying to formulate an argument against what she was being told to do. She felt as if she had just come racing around a corner and run smack-dab into herself.

Taking her eyes off her restless fingers, she was struck by how much Andrew had aged in the month since she'd taken over, and she wondered if he were ill. "Andrew, do we really care if Susie and Bill are having an affair?"

His eyes looked up from the quarter he'd been flipping up and down his knuckles. He glared at Kyla from under bushy brows. "It's against company policy. Period."

Those words, so reminiscent of her past, sent a stab of guilt to Kyla's stomach. But it wasn't the memory of Zach or the affair in Chicago behind the thrust. She wondered what Andrew would do if he learned she was currently violating another company policy by being involved in a telephone affair with the competition.

Telephone affair. How juvenile that sounded. It conjured up a vision of a young girl hanging on the phone while she painted her nails bright fuchsia and a Boy George tape played in the background. Not Kyla. She sat in silent darkness, no music to dilute the sensual rasp of Luke's voice. They shared their days, steering clear of Quantum and CompuMart as if they were potholes easily skirted. After exchanging events of the day, Luke fabricated dreams for the nights they spent alone. There was a strange cruelty in what they did to each other night after night, she thought.

She'd been toying with the idea of telling Andrew about the whole mess. The blossoming hope that he might tolerate an open relationship with Luke, trusting Kyla to keep the business part of her life separate from the personal, was being nipped in the bud at this very moment.

"Andrew, she's a receptionist and he's a regional manager. They can hardly pass confidential information to each other. What is the harm?"

She knew she was pushing the man's patience. But Kyla doubted she could summon the nerve to call either one of them in and self-righteously demand they stop seeing one another while *she* was involved in something that would be viewed as far more damaging to CompuMart.

"Of all people," Andrew admonished, "I wouldn't think you'd have to ask." He referred to Zach only because she'd pushed him to it. "These things happen. People share the same workplace eight hours a day; some are bound to be attracted to others. If it's possible, we turn our heads. But these two have moved in together."

Kyla could have gladly wrung Susie's neck for sending her new address down to accounting.

Couldn't she have arranged for the post office to forward her mail?

"I don't care who sleeps with whom," Andrew mumbled, clearly uneasy with the whole situation. "It's when they *stop* sleeping with each other we have to worry. People can be vicious when they're bitter. Fullerton should have taught you that. And that's the purpose of the policy. What, you may ask, could little Susie do to Bill if he dumps her? She could refuse to put his clients through to him when they call, transfer them to another salesman. She could hold his messages. What either of them does to the other hurts CompuMart in the final analysis."

"Susie? She wouldn't—"

Andrew's fist slammed down on her desk, effectively shutting Kyla's mouth. "It's policy. And a good one. If we shut our eyes to this because Susie doesn't have a malicious bone in her body, we have to shut our eyes to the next one. Then it'll be two regional managers having a lovers' spat, and we'll have one of those internal wars on our hands."

In five years, Andrew had never raised his voice to Kyla. But she deserved it this time and she knew it. "All right, Andrew. I'll talk to Bill."

At his astonished expression Kyla laughed, and the tension between them was diffused. "Oh, no. Not Susie. You know her, she'll blubber all over my office. I'd feel like an ax murderer."

"Company policy, Kyla," he grumbled on his way to the door.

"And it stinks," Kyla snapped back—after he'd closed the door behind him.

Bill wasn't in her office a full minute before he figured out why he'd been summoned. "I love her, Kyla. There isn't a job in the world worth losing Susie for."

"We didn't say anything for a long time, Bill. But she's moved in with you now. Couldn't you have made . . . other arrangements?"

"The lease on her apartment was up. She had to

sign for another year or get out. We're going to be married in a couple of months."

"Andrew is adamant. One of you has to go if the affair continues. Marriage isn't going to change his mind."

"She's looking for another job." Kyla's eyebrows shot up in surprise. "She didn't tell you. She didn't want you to replace her before she found something else."

"I won't do that, Bill. And I'll give her a good recommendation."

"Can you get Carson to lay off while she looks? Everybody and his brother has moved to California. Jobs are scarce. We can't hack it on one paycheck. Not yet."

"I'll talk to Andrew. And, Bill, in the meantime keep the kisses and the quarrels out of the office."

After Bill left, Kyla sat for a long time, distractedly running her fingertips in a circular pattern on her stomach. Then she realized she was subconsciously trying to soothe a deep, dark ache. Something Bill had said gnawed at her, like a rotten seed swallowed. *There isn't a job in the world worth losing Susie for.* She stood, pressing her temple to the window frame, and gazed out at the empty park bench across the street. If she were told tomorrow that she could have her job or have Luke, but never have both, she'd have to choose. That day was bound to come; she flirted with it every time she took his call. Where were they heading? There seemed to be only two possible directions—either he defeated her and became her boss, or he didn't defeat her and remained her rival. Either way . . .

Oh, it had been so much simpler when she hadn't been a vice-president and she'd thought he was unemployed. Kyla whirled away from the window suddenly. *Unemployed.* Why had she thought that? Because of something Luke had said in the mountains.

What do you do in Los Angeles? she'd asked.

In the civilized world, I'm a man in transition.

What had he meant? It had been an evasive answer at the time. But Luke didn't lie, not even to evade—there had to be truth behind it. Transition. Moving from one place to another. He hadn't meant homes. Kyla was positive the conversation had dealt with professions. She had to find out what he'd meant. There was a very real possibility . . .

Leaning forward, she pressed the intercom button and asked Martha to call Quantum and get Lucien Morainge on the phone for her. She didn't have the slightest idea how she'd ever explain why she was calling him if asked. And at the moment, she didn't much care.

"Gone for the day," Martha informed her a moment later. Kyla glanced at her wristwatch, surprised to see that it was after six o'clock. "I'll get his home number if you want that."

"No." Dammit, enough with phone calls. "See if you can get his address."

A few minutes later Kyla left CompuMart with Luke's street and house number clutched in her hand.

It hadn't been easy to find; she'd had to stop and ask directions three times. Kyla sat in her car in Luke's driveway, considering the sprawling redwood-sided house. It nestled beautifully in its foothill surroundings blending with the wooded lot.

With her heart thumping in her breast, she went up the front walk, suddenly wishing she'd thought to go home and change her clothes first. Her peasant skirt stubbornly held the wrinkles of the day. She'd embellished her limp white blouse with a fringed tangerine shawl, draped over one shoulder and tied at her waist. Catching her reflection in a window beside the door, she doubted this was how women dressed when they planned to seduce information from a man. This was so unlike her! *You'll use whatever you have to, if you have to.* Luke had told her that once. It seemed the time had come.

Just before putting her finger to the doorbell, she heard a splash and followed the sound around the side to the back of the house. Luke's blond head surfaced at one end of a long swimming pool. He began laps, doing the breaststroke. His long arms and broad shoulders rhythmically pounded the water; each implosion set off a sledgehammer response inside Kyla.

Feeling weak, she leaned against the side of the house, hidden well enough not to attract his attention. It had been nearly five weeks, and watching him quenched a certain thirst while stirring up another hunger.

"Missy!" an anxious female voice called to Kyla. "You get in here!" Kyla glanced across the stone terrace to see a large, aproned woman waving to her from a sliding glass door. "Get yourself in here, li'l girl. Quick now. He's gonna come bare-bottomed out of that water any minute."

Kyla smiled and began crossing the terrace. She'd have liked to stay for that, but she didn't think the militia, in the form of this woman, would allow it.

"He's a heathen boy," the woman grumbled as Kyla followed her into a huge, comfortable room. The house was exactly the kind she'd thought Luke would live in. Open. Rooms flowed from one to another, the colors were earthy and bold. Long, wide windows allowed the outdoors to be an integral part of the house. A place of residence without confinement, tucked away in the hills—halfway up the mountain, halfway to the city. A man, she thought, who seemed to have a foot in both worlds.

"You tell him the stew will be ready in twenty minutes." Kyla looked over to see the housekeeper, defrocked of her ruffled apron, with a hat on her head and a purse on her arm. "He didn't tell me he was having company, but there's enough for two. Now, you hide yourself till he gets dressed, hear? He'll prance about naked as the day he was born. Don't much care who sees him."

Kyla found the kitchen, amazed at the jungle of hanging plants. She saw the Crockpot with the stew on a counter and a baking tray with dinner rolls ready to pop in the oven next to it. She'd been tempted to go back to the pool and wait for Luke. But if he stepped naked out of the water, odds were Kyla would soon be in the same state—without getting the information she'd come for. For a woman who had faced the charge of using her feminine wiles to get ahead more than once, she was feeling quite ignorant of how it was done.

Gathering items for a salad from a well-stocked refrigerator, she began dicing ingredients at a chopping block, mentally choreographing the evening. His hand closed around her throat from behind, tipping her face up so their eyes met. Fringed by moisture-spiked lashes, his were the color of lush, velvety moss—eyes that begged her soul and could not be refused. Deep furrows lined his damp hair from his having run his fingers through it. The ends, beginning to curl, sparkled with water beads.

"I've been waiting for you," he murmured. "Night after night. Waiting. You're long overdue . . . but then, you're so damn stubborn."

It never occurred to her to question his certainty that eventually she'd come to him. Neither of them moved in the suspended time. They needed so much to look and see and adore. Kyla leaned in to his bare chest. Her thigh felt the soft barrier of towel between his legs, while her hands still loosely held a tomato and a paring knife.

"I never heard you come up behind me," Kyla whispered huskily. "You walk as quietly as a beast in search of prey."

Luke's hand at her neck began stroking while the other searched and removed the pins from her hair. "A doe bolts at the sound of her hunter. He learns to be very quiet."

"Don't . . . Luke . . . my hair . . ."

"When it's up, you're a city girl. I want my tenderfoot tonight."

Not until every strand had been combed free by his fingers did he finally bring his mouth to hers. Slowly, so very slowly, hovering a breath before touching, letting their eyes kiss first. Smooth, soft lips covered her parted mouth and warmth flooded her heart, flowing over into her veins. His tongue glanced off hers tentatively, sampling without haste. An endless kiss.

When he removed the items from her hands, Kyla knew things were moving too fast. If her pulse were any indication, they were moving *much* too fast. Luke put his arms around her waist, lifting her feet off the floor, and walked out of the kitchen.

"Uh . . . Luke, wait. Where are you taking me?"

"To bed."

"No." He'd crossed the living room and was moving down a long hall. "Your housekeeper . . . at least I think she's your housekeeper—"

"Gracie."

"Right. Gracie said to tell you the stew would be ready in twenty minutes . . . and that was about twenty minutes ago."

He stopped short of a closed door, turned on his heel, and retraced his steps. Relieved, Kyla rested her head on his shoulder. "Put me down, Luke. I can walk."

"Like hell I will."

He marched straight to the counter where the stew simmered. Holding Kyla with one arm, he pulled the plug on the Crockpot. Then he strode through the house again.

"Luke, I mean it! This isn't what I came for!"

"Like hell it isn't."

This time there was no stopping until he was through the door and standing in the center of a vast room where a decadently huge bed was draped by a navy-blue spread. When he set Kyla on her feet, she had a moment of vertigo and gasped a breath as she experienced the sensation of falling.

"Oh, Luke," she whispered in awe. "It's wonderful." The room appeared to be, or actually was, hanging in space. Two walls of glass came together at a ninety-degree angle to give a panoramic view of the city of Los Angeles. "It's like looking down from the top of a mountain."

When Kyla turned away from the breathtaking view the spread had been thrown back on the bed, Luke's towel lay in a pile on the floor, and Luke, sublimely naked, was walking toward her.

"No." The hand she threw out to stop him met with teasing, crisp chest hair. "Luke, I came to talk to you."

"Then you should have stayed home and waited for my call at ten."

His hands settled on her waist. His mouth moved on hers, shoving lucid thought aside. She heard the rasp of her skirt zipper being lowered and plastered her hands to her hips in time to catch the skirt before it fell. Luke swept the shawl from her shoulder to unfasten the buttons on her blouse. "Please, Luke. Do what I ask."

"I have, love. I've done what you asked until I think I'm going to die of it. I haven't seen you or touched you. I stopped following you. I stopped sending you flowers. I stopped helping you. Now I'm going to do everything I've only talked about doing."

She was aware of fewer clothes and soft air and a vague realization of having botched it as she stood there in revealing underwear. Luke picked her up and gently tumbled her to the bed. He came down beside her and she strove once more for a mental grip on sanity. Was it possible to garner information when you were vulnerably naked and a man was making love to you? Never! She could hardly breathe, let alone think!

"I'm going to cover every part of your gorgeous body I said I would touch." He released her bra clasp and slowly slid the straps down her arms . . . and smiled when Kyla held the lacy cups in place over her breasts. "I'm going to devour every sweet secret I said I would taste with my tongue." He peeled her hose down, taking her panties with them. "I'm going to adore every inch of you I said I would kiss."

Kyla's limbs turned to mush. Her arms easily fell away when Luke lifted them to bare her breasts. "Ah, love. I've missed you."

With his hands under her arms and spread across her back, he lifted her to the pillows piled at the headboard. The sun had set behind the twinkling lights of the city, washing a fiery glow over Luke's lean, sinewed body sprawled between Kyla's legs. He rubbed his face on the satin flesh at her waist and she watched in fascination as her hands frantically molded his back and shoulders.

His kisses took her breath away, inspired her instinctive responses. Sweet, warm touches of his mouth rediscovered her flesh, cherished the soft inside of her thighs. His breath stirred the dark down hiding that which he adored next. Mindlessly, Kyla groped the hands cupping her buttocks and carried them to her breasts.

She moaned, feeling the world slip away. His gentle plucks at her nipples, his curling, thrusting tongue, were all that existed. Whatever intentions had brought her here to him dissolved and washed away in the waves that broke through her.

Silken gold hair soothed her hot flesh as Luke grazed her skin with his lips until her breasts knew his mouth. Contentment filled her when he tugged at her nipple in restful suckling.

Drowsily at first, then boldly, Kyla explored his beloved body until, on a moan, her nipple slipped from his lips. She coaxed the same hard beads of his own nipples, the same spasms of delight, the same arch of implacable need, until he pulsed with pleasure.

He dragged her up the hard, muscled length of his body, and laid her down beneath him. "The flesh is satisfied," Luke managed raggedly. "Now the soul." He entered her slowly, with a long, deep stroke.

Their union was like no other they'd shared. Pleasure came second to fulfillment. Completion was a moment of suspension. Kyla did not soar up or crash down, but hovered on top of the world in the soft glow of a miracle . . . where she belonged.

"Luke?" Kyla lay curled to his side, her arms and legs draped over his hard body.

"Hmm?"

"When we made love you mentioned the flesh and the soul. Why didn't you mention the heart?"

Luke tipped her chin up, dropping a kiss on her forehead. "My heart has been content these last weeks. It has loved you. And that's all a heart needs."

Yes, Kyla thought with a sigh, that is all a heart needs—to love. It is the soul that needs to be loved back, and the flesh to know that love.

"Now, tenderfoot. Why don't you ask me whatever it was you came here to seduce from me."

Kyla scrambled to a sitting position. "What!"

"Don't act so indignant, love. You know I'm right. Out with it."

Her cheeks burned with embarrassment. "Am I that transparent?"

"Let's just say the femme fatale is not your strong role."

Feeling sufficiently piqued, Kyla tossed back, "I'll have to practice it, then."

Soft bunches of hair tumbling down her shoulders were curled in his fists, and she was pulled back down to lie on his chest. Their eyes flashed flame and emerald. "No need, love. You will seduce no one but me. And if you want information from me, you have only to ask."

With a sigh, Kyla tore her eyes away and rested her cheek on his chest, seeking the rhythm of his heartbeat. "I came here to find out what you meant when you told me in the mountains you were a man in transition."

"Exactly that. In one place but going to another."

"What are you moving from?"

"Quantum."

Kyla's heart seemed to stand still. It was true, then. He was leaving them. She tried to think what her next question should be, when Luke slid away from her and left the bed. He strolled to a closet, returning with two bathrobes. Shrugging into chocolate-brown terrycloth, he held a short black satin kimono out to Kyla.

"Come on, love. The stomach is feeling neglected."

"What will you be moving to?" she asked, feeling a tarnished happiness at his confirmation of her suspicions, but unsure what had come along to dull the shine.

"My own company. A venture-capital firm."

"A moneyman?" Kyla gasped. Her astonishment was sincere, but without censure. She sat in the middle of the bed, raking her hair back. Her hands stilled in a pose that made her look as if she were trying to hold her head together. Had he said he planned to lose himself in the mountains and open a lumber camp, she'd have understood. She wouldn't have liked it, but she'd have understood. "A capitalist?" she breathed.

"A dream-maker," Luke countered.

Kyla considered that aspect of it. "Backing inventors. Like your father."

"Could we continue this discussion in the kitchen while I see if I can salvage any of that stew?"

Kyla curled up in a chair at the kitchen table. Black satin cuffs drooped over the wineglass she swirled. Luke moved around the kitchen, telling her of two young men in Phoenix who had made a phenomenal discovery in the field of robotics. There were others, too, that excited him, particularly one nontechnical firm—the sort rarely considered for venture capital. The specifics failed to register with Kyla; she was too aware of the animation in Luke's face, the sensual shape of his relaxed mouth, the soft brilliance in his eyes. How incredibly happy he looked, she thought, wishing she felt the same.

When he took the seat across from her and set down the food, Kyla tried to give it full effort but only came up with halfhearted enthusiasm.

"Let's see," Luke interrupted her distracted thoughts. "I know you eat everything in sight when you're nervous. And push your plate away when you're angry. What does it mean when you play with your food and pretend to eat?"

Kyla dropped her fork to the dish with a clatter. "If you're leaving Quantum to start your own company, why are you still trying to destroy mine?"

He took one look at her eyes, at the fires there, and laid down his own fork to cross his arms over his chest. "Because acquiring CompuMart is the only way Quantum will release me from a five-year contract. It's my ticket out."

Kyla blinked, thunderstruck. "Explain. In detail."

"Two years ago Quantum went public, trading on the stock exchange. And from that day forward they've made me a hatchet man, weeding out the glut in the marketplace by cutting down the little guy. I hate it. They were all competent people, as you are but no match for me. I don't mean in ability or intelligence. My edge is the stockholders' money; I can put on a squeeze and hold longer. It's not my nature to destroy, Kyla. I'm a . . . a . . . ."

"A nurturer," Kyla said.

He rubbed the tips of his fingers down the slope of her jaw, but Kyla's remoteness only seemed to grow. "I've trained a successor. The board of directors is very satisfied with him. However, their concern is that an announcement of a new president, when it's known I have five years to go, will cause some sell-off by investors." He sighed heavily. "Quantum is presently overrated on the market. It could have nasty long-term effects.

"So you see, they'd prefer to hold me to my contract. They're only willing to let me go if I guarantee stockholder confidence. With the right timing, I can leave at the first of the quarter. A tremendous order shortly after will give the new president a stunning quarterly report and that should keep the trust of the investors."

"Hi-Life."

"Hi-Life."

"Have I thrown your timing off, Luke?"

He shrugged. "Somewhat, love."

Long seconds passed. Kyla heard the ticking of the clock on the wall, the call of a bird outside the window, the screech of tires rounding a corner. "I think I'd like to go home now."

"Kyla—"

"Really, Luke. I came for information I thought I needed, wanted . . . and I find I'd have been better off not knowing. A real Pandora's box."

Luke caught her at the bedroom door. When he turned her around, her cheeks were bathed with tears. "What, Kyla? Tell me."

"This is your dream, isn't it? To back inventors. To give others the break your father never had. And the only person standing in your way is me. If I don't back down, you'll be sentenced to five more years with a company that . . . that puts that awful caged look in your eyes. I can set the eagle free if I compromise my boss, my company, myself."

He watched her dress and walked with her to the door, where he wrapped her in the bonds of his arms and held her. "What we *have* with each other is love. What we *do* to each other is—"

"Business," she said stiffly. But she didn't believe it anymore. What they did to each other affected what they had.

Kyla sat across from Andrew Carson's desk, dreading the ensuing conversation. She set her interlaced hands in her lap and met Andrew's eyes. "Quantum Company is actively seeking to acquire CompuMart." He looked stunned. She let the full impact sink in before going on.

It took her over an hour to relate the whole story, starting with Hi-Life and National Office Supply, and to answer the questions Andrew interspersed. The personal aspect was deftly neglected without Kyla having to lie about it. Andrew accepted that, when things came to a head, Kyla had arranged to have dinner with Lucien Morainge. She saw no reason to mention where that dinner had taken place.

After long and thoughtful contemplation of the ceiling, Andrew surprised Kyla with his suggestion. "Why don't they simply make me an offer?"

"Buy you out?"

"Why not? Morainge doesn't seem to have the time to get me cheap . . . he needs me now. For the Hi-Life orders. Who am I going to leave it to? I have no children." Kyla received his words like physical blows. "This is my company. My life's effort. I don't want to see it run down to nothing so they can take it over. Let them buy it. Let me go out with some dignity."

"I see." He never considered she might save it for him, she thought regretfully.

"See what sort of deal you can get me."

"Me?"

"Yes, you. There'll be offers, counteroffers. You take care of all that. When the deal is solid, then bring me into it."

Kyla walked back to her office in a daze. She had never expected this. "Martha." She noticed that her lips moved strangely, as if they were numb. "Will you get Lucien Morainge of Quantum Company on the phone for me?"

Kyla sat at her desk staring at the button on her phone, waiting for it to glow—like the eye of the enemy.

"Hello, love."

"Good morning, Mr. Morainge. Andrew Carson has asked me to meet with you and come to mutually agreeable terms for the sale of CompuMart to Quantum. Would you care to make an appointment to meet with me?"

He was silent for a moment. "Kyla, are you okay?" When she didn't respond, he said, "Over dinner at my house, tonight."

"I'm afraid that wouldn't be appropriate, Mr. Morainge. This is strictly business."

Eleven

Luke was already at the corner table when Kyla
arrived. They had been meeting in restaurants—
neutral territory—for nearly two weeks. These were
the only times they saw each other. And this is the
last meeting, Kyla thought, wending her way to the
table. Except for tomorrow at the bank. Then it will be
official. And over.

"I ordered for you," Luke said, smiling as she slid
into the booth across from him. It didn't matter that
she rarely returned them anymore, he always had a
smile for her. But then, he was the victor, she
thought. Why shouldn't he be feeling good?

"I don't think I can eat anything, thanks." Kyla
slipped out of her black bolero jacket and draped it on
the seat next to her. Her hot pink blouse was a lively
splash of color in the somber dining room. She placed
a stack of papers down near his elbow. "If you'll look
those over, please. I think I've solved the problem of
the Opticillusion sales. The first delivery arrived this
morning, by the way. Only ten days late."

"The splits are fair?" Luke glanced at the terri
172

tory map Kyla had color-coded. With salespeople from both companies selling the same product in overlapping regions, it had been necessary to find a fair and equal way of assigning areas that would be commission-fair.

"There'll be some who will cry foul, but we knew that. It's as fair as I could make it." A bowl of onion soup was set down in front of Kyla.

"Eat it," Luke commanded. "It's all I ordered for you, but it's something. If you don't start eating, you'll make yourself sick."

"In any case," Kyla continued, placating the stern emerald eyes by taking a sip of her soup, "whoever is in charge can clean up territory problems later. The deal certainly isn't going to hinge on who sells where. Which brings me to the next item. Andrew respectfully declines your offer to let him continue as president of CompuMart."

"I figured he would," Luke said.

It had been thoughtful of Luke to make that part of the package, she thought, and respectful of Andrew. CompuMart would continue to operate out of the same offices and building, keep its name and a good deal of its staff. Changes in titling would be minimal—the stationery would now read: "Compu-Mart, a subsidiary of Quantum Company." The executive staff was as yet unchosen. Luke and Kyla both felt the new president should be able to make those decisions, with the parent company's approval, of course.

"I could always stick Brad Upton in there," Luke said. The aggravation in his voice brought the first real smile to Kyla's lips.

"How is Brad doing for you?"

"A whole lot of starting, but no finish. You stuck me with that one, love. I can count his loyal clients on one hand. He didn't bring us enough business to justify his percentages."

Kyla's smile slipped away. She needed an emotional freeze; it was her best protection against hating him. She didn't want that. "It's moot, isn't it? You got the whole kit and caboodle anyway."

Luke pressed his lips against whatever comeback had sprung to his mind and returned to the business at hand. They went over arrangements on pension plans, insurance programs, life-insurance policies, which employees to keep, who had to be let go. After two weeks of negotiations, Kyla believed they had done what was best for everyone. Both of them had held firm on some issues, both of them had had to give in on others. But Luke had been fair.

"Damn those eyes. Kyla, will you stop looking at me like I killed your grandmother?"

She made a cursory stab at a smile. "You want me to grin and bear it? Why? So you can feel better? Why should either one of us feel good or bad? After all, you did say this was only business."

He cursed and threw his napkin on the table. Kyla was not going to get into a discussion of ethics, semantics, or business practices. She knew acquisitions happened all the time. She knew she shouldn't take it personally. Still, it hurt, and the wound was fresh. She picked up her jacket and purse from the seat beside her and started to slide out of the booth.

Luke trapped her foot between his legs under the table. A small smile played with the edges of his mouth. "You're not planning to bolt, are you, tenderfoot?"

"Let go of my foot, Luke," Kyla snapped.

"Or what?"

"Or I'll free it myself and— "

"I know . . . ram it through my pocket."

Kyla slumped to the back of the leather booth. "What do you want?"

"I want you to start looking at this realistically."

"Realistically," Kyla murmured, testing the word. She looked at Luke and let herself see him, something she hadn't allowed during these sessions. Sleep came easier if he wasn't bronze flesh, gold mane, and jade eyes. The essence and vision of him had been filtered through her pain until he was reduced to "the opponent's position."

Now she let herself see him. Navy suit. Pale blue shirt. Silver-and-maroon striped tie. Disheveled hair. Drumming fingers. Soft eyes. Firm mouth. Expectant.

"I've looked at some new realities lately," Kyla informed him coolly. "The first reality I faced was that you were never at risk. I should be grateful you cared enough about my position not to flaunt our relationship. For all my fears on your behalf as well as my own—you had nothing to lose. If we'd been discovered and fired, you'd have been set free, I'd have been ruined. But that wouldn't have happened to you. Quantum wanted too badly to keep you." Kyla looked at her hands, which were calmly resting on the table. "Did you laugh at me, Luke? I was as skittish in the city as I was in the mountains, jumping at every little noise, looking for extinct bears in the woods. And you never had anything to lose, while I had everything."

"And that's my fault?" His jaw jutted with righteousness, until he faced the suffering in her eyes. "Of course I never laughed at you, love."

"Another reality I had to face was the reason I went to Andrew when I did." She took a shaky breath. "Because I was a coward. And I'd never thought that of myself in terms of my work. Suddenly I was pulled between two loyalties. Instead of handling it regardless of what it demanded, regardless of the outcome, I dumped it in someone else's lap."

"Andrew *owns* CompuMart. He had every right to know what was going on."

"But that isn't why I went to him. I felt . . ." She closed her eyes and shook her head. "I felt just like I did when I had to cross that rift in the mountain. Wanting to go down, knowing I'd be a quitter, but a safe, alive quitter." She opened her eyes and gave him a cynical smile. "I walked across that tree because I felt I owed it to you. Not to get to the top, but because it seemed to have hurt you physically to cut the maple down, and you'd done it for me."

"What difference does it make why? You got to the top. You made it."

"Not this time, Luke." She gave a bitter little laugh. "Ironic, isn't it? In the physical world, I didn't give up. But here in my world I folded."

"Kyla, dammit! You said yourself Andrew looks bad, that he might be ill. This is what *he* wants."

"Because he didn't think I could outmaneuver you. And neither did you, Luke. You didn't believe in me. You thought you had to help me, guide me, every step of the way." She blinked the tears back, determined not to cry. "This was my life, what I've spent all of my adult years doing. I could have taken it from a stranger. But not from the man who took me to the top of a mountain and made me whole. I'm in pieces again, Luke. You stole my confidence . . . you cut me down."

Kyla tore her eyes from his face. It was rigidly set, but she saw the subtle effects of anguish in his pinched mouth and too-bright eyes. It was never her intention to cause him pain. She knew how he hated to destroy anything. Sliding her hand into the pocket of her skirt, she drew out his gold cuff link. It had lain in so many pockets, where she could touch it and somehow be linked to him. She placed it on the table. "This is yours. You lost it in . . . in my hotel room in San Francisco." She picked up the check and gathered her belongings. "Lunch is on me. I believe I still owe you forty dollars? Now we're even."

Sometime during the last few minutes, he had released her foot, and Kyla got up to go. Halfway across the room she heard, "See you soon, Kyla."

Yes, she thought tiredly, tomorrow at the bank. And then it would be over. Finished. The hunter had lifted his rifle, put it to his shoulder, and fired. Tomorrow he would carry off the carcass.

Kyla wore a dark burgundy suit to the bank. The severity of the tailored style, so neat and somber, was very unlike her usual outfits. Appropriate for a funeral, she thought.

The Quantum contingent filed into the private room where Kyla, Andrew, and Vince were already waiting. Kyla turned from where she stood at the far side of the room, expecting to see Luke. But he wasn't among them. Coward, she thought. *Dammit, you coward!* How dare he not be around for the finish. Predators should have to watch their victims' final hour, she thought bitterly.

A man introduced as Harvey Bockman, the man Luke had trained to succeed him, explained that he would be handling the final paperwork. Andrew went over the financial arrangements with the bank representative and his lawyer. Kyla and Vince glanced through the final managerial points she and Luke had ironed out.

"The only thing left to finalize," Bockman said, "is CompuMart's president. There has to be a boss Monday morning," he quipped. A few strained chuckles joined him in laughter. "Ms. Trent recently informed Mr. Morainge that you, Mr. Carson, are not interested. Am I correct?"

Andrew smiled, lifting his eyes from the legal papers. "That's right, Harvey, I'll sit this one out. I'm ready to look into watercolors."

Kyla wanted to cry, remembering their late-night discussions in the office.

"I'm surprised Mr. Morainge isn't here today," Kyla said, mentioning it only because Bockman had brought his name up.

"He's already left."

"He's left Quantum?" Kyla asked. "Isn't that a lit-tle sudden?"

"Oh, no, not Quantum. That will take some time yet; lots of ends to tie up, you know. I meant, he's left for the weekend. Gone up to the mountains. He said he had to give back what's been taken away." A look of bafflement creased the man's face. "I believe he intends to plant a tree?"

Kyla smiled sadly. Yes, Luke would do that. Replace the maple he'd cut down.

"But to get back to the issue. Mr. Morainge has advised us that Ms. Trent is the most qualified person to assume the presidency of CompuMart." Kyla blinked. She? "He knows of no other person better qualified. You have the full support of the Quantum board of directors. Mr. Morainge presented your cre-dentials at the board meeting last week in the event Mr. Carson declined. Are you interested in the posi-tion, Ms. Trent?"

Kyla nodded, feeling numb all over. She hadn't expected it. In fact, she'd wondered if she would have to fight the new president to keep the position she already had. The conversation swirled around her as she tried to come to grips with this.

He said he had to give back what's been taken.

She pressed her fingers to her lips. She would not cry! Not here. Typical female, these men would say, you can't even give them promotions without turning on the waterworks. They wouldn't know these were tears of joy at being given back her life. The joy of being whole again.

The first snows of the season had fallen in the mountains. Kyla got out of her car and slammed the door. The sound was a brittle crack in the cold air, bringing Jake out of the back door of his store.

"Beth," he called inside. "Come see who's here! Luke's girl!"

Kyla shoved her hands into the pockets of her suede jacket and smiled. That sounded nice, very nice: Luke's girl. "Can I leave my car here, Jake? It won't make it down the road to Luke's."

"Sure, sure. I'll take you there in my pickup," Jake offered.

"No, thanks. I'd prefer to walk."

She set out, finding the path under the thin layer of powder. The leaves were off the trees higher up the mountain, but the pines here were as full and abundant as ever, hanging a little lower to hug the cottage roofs under their burden of snow. She heard the sound of the shovel scraping in and out of the earth.

His back was to her as he worked to forge a hole in the ground. A young maple sapling lay on the ground near him, its balled roots protected in a burlap wrap. Kyla sat on a fallen tree trunk, elbows on knees, chin in palms, and watched him. It could prove to become a favorite pastime, she thought happily—he was still the best scenery around. Pale sunlight washed his light hair, glowed on his tanned flesh. The straining muscles of his back were hidden by his thick sheepskin coat. But jeans worn thin covered his legs and Kyla relished studying the brace and release of powerful muscles. He never once turned around as she watched him deepen the hole, set the tree in and stand it straight, then cover it up. When he was finished, he stabbed the shovel into the ground.

"I've been waiting for you," he said. Then he glanced over his shoulder at her.

Kyla stood up and went to him, reaching for his face with her hands, caressing his beautiful features with her fingertips. "How did you know I was there?"

"I always know where you are. You carry my heart with you."

Tears slipped over her lower lashes and plopped hotly to her cheeks. Luke lifted them with the tip of his finger. "Don't cry out here in the cold, come inside where it's warm."

Kyla hugged him around the waist as they walked to the front door of his parents' cabin. Inside, a fire was roaring in the hearth and Kyla saw a table set for two, a couple of steaks on the kitchen counter, and a bottle of champagne on ice with two glasses next to it.

"You really have been waiting for me."

"All of my life, love. I'd nearly given up finding you. And then you turned from Pop's window and I knew I'd found that little bit of wild beauty that was mine."

She threw herself into his arms and kissed him, knowing she'd come home. "I'm so sorry, Luke. For the things I said yesterday. For hurting you with them. Why didn't you tell me about the presidency?"

"Sh, sh." His hands cradled her neck, his thumbs urging her face up. He covered her lips with his, warming them, and welcoming her. Kyla's hands plunged into his hair, which was damp with the melting snow. "Can we get rid of this?" He slid her jacket off, then removed his own. "I thought about telling you yesterday. But you were in this strange mood, throwing everything I said back in my face. Being the stubborn woman that you are, I was afraid you'd tell me to put the presidency where you didn't put your foot."

"Mmm, yes. In your pocket." She rested her cheek on his chest, rubbing her face contentedly in the warmth of him.

His eyes were soft with love as he pulled her under his arm and walked her toward the hearth. "What do you think of the name Hudson?"

Kyla frowned in confusion. "I've always liked the name."

"I mean, how do you like the name Kyla Hudson? As in Luke and Kyla Hudson. I'm going to have it legally changed."

"Isn't that complicated, Luke? You'd have to change all your ID, notify so many people . . ."

"Must be the hair," he muttered, and began plucking the pins free. "Such a businesswoman when your hair is up. And that's a lousy way to answer my proposal of marriage."

"It was a lousy proposal. You were much more creative at propositioning me into beds and onto mountains."

Luke combed the wild strands that refused to be tamed. "You want the whole treatment?"

"Mm-hmm."

"Okay." He pulled her down to the carpet in front of the fire, both of them reclining on chintz pillows propped against a sofa. After nestling her in his arms, he said, "Kyla Trent, will you come share my world? Put lotion on my blisters and build my fires? Make love and babies with me? Climb mountains and go to the top with me? Feed my heart and soul and flesh? For as long as we both shall live?"

"Yes, Luke Hudson, I will." She touched his lips softly with her fingers. "I love you." Then replaced her fingers with her mouth.

"A whole new beginning." He raised himself above her. "Calls for champagne. Stay where you are. Don't move while I get it."

Kyla sat up, pulling her sweater over her head, the crackle of static as the wool rushed down her hair echoing the electric desire filling her. As Luke returned with the tray of champagne and glasses, he saw her and stopped. She sat naked in the fire's glow, her eyes big and pleading, her hair wildly tumbling to the floor. He set the tray down and came to her, stripping off his clothes before dropping to his knees.

"Didn't your mother teach you to wear clothes?" he demanded throatily.

"Oh, yes," Kyla murmured, linking her arms around his waist as she lay back on the floor. "Eight layers thick." She laughed softly, a deep womanly sound that drew a rough groan from Luke. "But that was before I met a mountain man who taught me to be wonderfully uncivilized."

His body responded to the soft flesh immediately. "You're throwing my timing off, love," he complained in strained tremors. Sitting back on his heels, he looked down on her. "The champagne is supposed to come first."

Kyla sat up, smiling. "I think we can negotiate this." With her hands on his shoulders, she lifted herself to sit on his thighs, wrapping her legs around his lean waist. Taking the champagne glasses from the tray, she handed one to Luke.

His trembling fingers accepted the glass. "Are you sure you know what you're doing?"

"Trust me, I'm a pro." Then she fitted her body to his with an easy uplift of her hips, whispering softly in his ear, "Is everybody happy?"

"Ecstatic," Luke groaned, then clinked his glass against hers. "To a merger made in the mountains."

"To partners," Kyla answered.

THE EDITOR'S CORNER

You can plunk down right in your own living room and take four glorious vacations next month. Our LOVE-SWEPTS for August will take you from coast to coast and from north to south.

First, we have the delightful West Coast setting of Nancy Holder's **OUT OF THIS WORLD**, LOVESWEPT #103. Raucous, uproarious and truly tender, **OUT OF THIS WORLD** is the story of a young actress, Janet Madison, who has become a television phenomenon as Kalinda, Queen of the Galaxy, and Gary Wolf, the network exec who holds the fate of her series in his hands. Janet and Gary meet at a science fiction convention—a wild and woolly scene, if there ever was one—and there's conflict of interest, wills, and wants right from the start. You've met Janet before, remember? She was the best friend of the heroine of **FINDERS KEEPERS,** Nancy's last—and warmly received—LOVESWEPT. So, remembering the some-what kooky and definitely warm-hearted Janet, you'll be certain that her love story is one you just can't afford to miss!

Next, in **SUSPICION,** LOVESWEPT #104, our mar-velous new author Millie Grey will take you to sunny climes (Puerto Rico and Florida) with her romance between Cade Hamilton and Lita Jamison. This vivid and dramatic tale is certainly appropriately titled. **SUSPICION** draws Cade to Lita . . . then forces him to be emotionally distant from her. He believes the worst of her: that she shot his brother. Still, he finds himself falling passionately and deeply in love with

(continued)

her. But Lita, discovering his false beliefs about her, is hurt and humiliated—though just as much in love with Cade as he is with her. Only by laying to rest all their **SUSPICION** can they find joyous fulfillment. We think you're going to be captivated by Millie Grey's powerful storytelling and vivid style of writing.

Now, armchair traveler, prepare to journey to the East Coast, Boston to be exact, for Joan Elliott Pickart's humorous and touching romance, **THE SHADOWLESS DAY,** LOVESWEPT #105. Linc Reynolds is a dream of a hero: supremely self-confident, high-powered but soft-hearted, and a masterful lover. But Barbara Drake resists all Linc's potent charm as she persists in hiding away from emotional tugs and commitments. Linc pursues her until she surrenders all but her past. Then, torn, Barbara must choose between a safe life that casts no shadow or risking a new dream in Linc's arms. **THE SHADOWLESS DAY** is the latest in Joan's string of memorable LOVESWEPTS, but certainly not her last!

Finally, on the itinerary is a quick trip south to good ol' Mississippi for **TAMING MAGGIE,** LOVESWEPT #106, by our charming new writer, Peggy Webb. Clever, zippy, sizzling, and touching, **TAMING MAGGIE** chronicles the romance of tender-hearted Maggie Merriweather and impossibly virile Adam Trent. Maggie and Adam were destined to be adversaries from the moment they met . . . at the opening of duck hunting season. Maggie was at the river at dawn with her silver trumpet in hand to scare away the birds; Adam was concealed in a blind, gun in hand, happily anticipating a roast duck dinner that night! Suddenly the fight was on . . . and you have a ringside seat as these two lovable people discover the compromises they must make to triumph over their differences.

Happy vacation days with next month's LOVE-SWEPTS.

All best wishes,

Carolyn Nichols

Carolyn Nichols
  Editor
LOVESWEPT
Bantam Books, Inc.
666 Fifth Avenue
New York, NY 10103

*In a world of high stakes and fast living,
everything she wanted had a price . . .*

RECKLESS DREAMER

by Dion Alden

Beautiful talented photographer Alison Carmichael
yearned for love and the power to shape her own
destiny, but pursuing her dream threw her into
the arms of three men who would change her life
forever: Alain, the idealistic French student who
awakened her to womanhood in Paris, where she
learned the stunning power of the camera's eye;
Kenny, the aspiring rock singer who wanted star-
dom at any cost; and Sam, the wealthy Texan
whose driving ambition more than matched her
own . . .

Sweeping from the Paris of romantic dreams to
the glitter and ruthlessness of the Hollywood film
world to the lush playgrounds of the super-rich,
RECKLESS DREAMER is the story of one woman's passionate odyssey from desperation to triumph.

Turn the page for a preview of Dion Alden's RECK-
LESS DREAMER, coming in August 1985 from
Bantam Books.

RECKLESS DREAMER
by Dion Alden

Click! Click!

Alison Carmichael kept snapping the shutter of the
Leica.

*One more shot! And then another! And another! Hold
it! Yes! This may be the perfect photo.*

It was spring. It was Paris. The chestnut trees were in
blossom just as the song said. And Alison Carmichael was
very young and very beautiful, and totally unaware of the
devastating effect she was having on Parisians. Right now
she couldn't take enough photographs. Around every street
corner there was something new and dazzling. Circus
posters exploding against the medieval gray walls of the
Latin Quarter. Bunches of flowers sunning themselves on
windowsills. She only had eyes for these images, and the
passersby only had eyes for her.

Alison had the long leggy look of a thoroughbred and
could have been mistaken for a fashion model. Whatever
she wore acquired an incredible chic, mainly because she
wore it. Maybe it was due to the high cheekbones and the
clear blue eyes, gifts from her father. Or the delicacy of
her other features—her mother's gifts. Quite possibly it
was her hair, which was the color of honey. It had been
streaked by the sun on Vermont ski slopes in winter and
salted by the spray on the centerboard sloops that left the
Marblehead Yacht Club every careless summer Sunday

afternoon. Jonathan Carmichael's estate was at Pride's Crossing, Massachusetts, ten miles from the yacht club.

Alison's look was all of these things, and one thing more. She wore clothes with the carelessness of people born to money.

At nineteen she was totally unaware of anything that she did not find by looking into the camera. Actually she had always been that way, from the time her father gave her her first camera on her seventh birthday. She had peered through the viewfinder and loved the world she saw there. It was a clear, focused world with well-defined boundaries.

She had taken her camera with her everywhere. She had gone to the correct New England preparatory school, the correct New England college, attended the correct coming-out parties, and survived the weekends at Yale. She had applied for admission to the Sorbonne for her third year of college. One day in the spring of 1967 there was a letter of acceptance in her mailbox. She would attend the School of Photography and Fine Arts in Paris.

All that fall and winter, when she wasn't in class or in the darkroom, she wandered through Paris, camera always at hand. She shot for the Decisive Moment. She either got it or she got nothing. But like gunmen in the Old West, she learned to shoot fast.

She photographed Versailles, the Hall of Mirrors and the glorious paintings. Under the guise of mythology, of Hercules and Apollo, the plushest of kings and rosiest of females cavorted, while beneath them the real Louis XIV and his court gambled and gamboled, chattered and connived, until two Louis later it was all swept away in the Revolution of 1789. All those pretty birds of paradise with their heads chopped off by the guillotine, stripped of their ribbons and silks and lace and plumage and thrown into wagons and dumped into ditches. Still left were the gardens, the buildings, the grandeur of Fontainebleau and the palace of Versailles.

But another revolution was brewing.

On a Friday afternoon, as cold and mean as May can be in Paris, the head of the Sorbonne was forced to call in the Paris police to clear the university courtyard of a small and disputatious student meeting. Violating the sanctuary of the courtyard, of the university—something which had been maintained for centuries—brought about a protest. Violence exploded when students and some of the professors saw other students being hauled off to a police station. By Saturday night there was marching in the streets. By Sunday morning ten students were dead, fifteen hundred wounded. Several students had been sentenced to two years in prison. The news whizzed through the university like the bullets of snipers. Within hours the entire student body along with some members of the Sorbonne had risen in a fury.

Overnight the City of Light became the City of Outrage. The workers, eight million of them, almost half the labor force, joined the students. Paris was all but immobilized by strikes. Suddenly there was no more mail delivery. No newspapers. The telephone service was sporadic. Workers took over their factories. There were demonstrations every day and every night. Conflicts erupted between groups. Cars were overturned and set on fire. The Latin Quarter blossomed with slogans. SOYONS CRUELS—"Let us be cruel"—was painted on the walls of the Sorbonne. Young students, armed with garbage-pail covers and wearing white masks splashed with red paint to protest the bloodied faces of their comrades, confronted the elite and despised Compagnies Républicaines de Sécurité, who wore futuristic anti-tear gas goggles and were armed with truncheons and tear gas.

The students built huge barricades from cobblestones. The C.R.S. tossed in the tear gas. The students fled, running up the staircases of the houses. They began fighting from the roofs, tipping parapet stones onto the enemy below. Some members of the C.R.S. indiscriminately pursued, arrested, beat anyone in the streets. Students, workers, bystanders. Men, women, children.

And through it all, somewhat as though she were on a summer-camp tour and therefore not susceptible to injury or violence, Alison floated, snapping pictures, catching in her camera the faces of the impassioned students; the horror of the onlookers; the bewilderment of the bourgeoisie, whose tranquil world had just exploded; the anger of the police; the viciousness of class hatred; the glowering hostility of the workers. It was all there. Exultation, passion, sorrow, death, resolution.

For two weeks the revolution continued to rip the country apart, to threaten the government of Charles de Gaulle. There was very little sleeping at night, and during the day one roamed the streets, never sure what was around the next corner. A demonstration? A roundup?

Therefore it was not surprising when, late one evening, Alison heard the racing of feet up and down the hallway outside her apartment. There were cries and muffled curses, commands and commotion, and then a pounding on her door.

It frightened her. The pounding was so insistent, so desperate. At first she kept quiet. Perhaps they would go away. But they did not. The pounding continued.

"Who is it? What do you want?" she called out. Her voice sounded tiny.

"*Ouvre la porte!*" came the cry from outside. It was a man. It sounded like a young man, a frightened man.

She overcame her own fear and undid the latch. A boy of eighteen pushed his way in, proceeded to the kitchen sink, and began washing his hands. There was tar from the paving blocks on his dirty fingers. His dirty fingers would convict him.

"*T'es pas française. . . .*" he whispered at her, lacking breath. Alison shook her head no.

"*Anglaise? Américaine?*"

"*Américaine,*" she said.

He had time for one more word. "Help!" he said, wiping the dirty black ringlets from his forehead and lighting a cigarette.

There came a second knock on the door.

"*Police!*" Another angry rap. Again Alison opened the door. Immediately there was a babble of French that she only half comprehended. She pretended she understood nothing at all.

"What is it? Why are you here?" she asked.

"*Américaine?*" the policeman questioned her.

Alison reached for her bag. Miraculously she found her passport. She held it up in front of her as one held a cross before a vampire. It would, she felt, protect her from all evil.

The agent examined the passport, returned it, and nodded in the direction of the young man.

"*Et lui?*" he asked.

A phrase came to her, though she wasn't sure why.

"Make love, not war," she said, and smiled. The agent looked at her curiously and then at the boy.

"*Faire l'amour, pas la guerre,*" the boy translated, then added, "*C'est du Viêt-nam.*"

The officer looked at their hands. Clean hands. Unpolitical hands. He left. She closed the door and bolted it, then turned around.

"*Merci,*" the boy said, and Alison merely nodded. She felt she had run ten miles. She was gasping for breath and her hands were shaking.

"*Calme-toi,*" the boy reassured her, and smiled. Then, in English, he said, "It's okay." The word sounded ridiculous but charming. There was something in his tone and manner that made Alison feel everything *would* be okay.

"Whatever is going to happen?" she asked tentatively. "Can we continue this in English? At least till I get my bearings."

"Okay," the boy repeated, and grinned. "This was something, *hein?* You never experience this . . . thrill . . . of danger before?"

"No. I guess I always kept my distance."

"Kept your distance?" The words confused him.

"Kept away. To myself." She was floundering. He lit another cigarette.

"That is too bad. 'To keep to oneself,' " he said mockingly. "It is better to be involved." There was a gentle insinuation in his voice that made her look at him.

Under the dirt and exhaustion that came from two weeks of street fighting, he was handsome, Alison noticed—. and perhaps more a man than a boy. He was dark, with dark brown eyes, his hair snarled now but naturally curly.

He had not shaved in two or three days, and his face was pale. She looked at his hands. They were strong; the veins stood out. She gathered that he was powerful, although slight.

"Shall I go?" he asked. His eyes were amused. He seemed to be reading her mind.

"No, not just yet," she said, flustered.

"You are alone here?" he asked.

"Yes. I live alone."

"You keep to yourself."

"Yes. So far." He blinked. He was on the verge of collapse.

"Stay the night. It will be all right," Alison said impulsively.

His smile was self-mocking. "Ah, yes, you will be safe tonight," he said, and looked for a place to lie down. What he saw was not encouraging. Three chairs and a table in the living room, and in the bedroom only the bed and the dresser.

He started to lie down on the floor.

"Take the bed," she said. "I'm not sleepy. I can sleep in the chair if I feel like it."

He was too tired to protest. He nodded his thanks and headed for the bedroom. He lay down on the bed and was asleep immediately.

Alison watched him for a moment. She could not believe what she had done. Who was this young man she had let in? Who was *she*? She was suddenly someone she could not recognize. What kind of behavior was this?

Outside the crashing of glass and the sound of sirens continued. Shouts and cries carried through the darkened streets. Periodically she could hear the sound of running feet. Another chase.

The boy slept on.

The next morning Alison made coffee. She offered the man a cup, and he told her his name was Alain. When she learned he had no place to stay that night, she suggested shyly he stay with her. He accepted, kissed her on the cheek, and was gone.

It was as though he had never been there—except for the feel of his lips on her cheek. She put her hand there. He had given her such a casual kiss, the most casual kind of kiss, and for some reason she just stood in the middle of the room, stunned and breathless.

She felt dizzy. Was she in love? she wondered. In love with a boy whose first name was Alain, and whose last name she did not know? He lived somewhere outside of Paris. He was involved in *les événements*. They had spoken only maybe twenty sentences to each other.

First dizzy and then exhilarated, she tried to eat a croissant but wasn't hungry. She could not forget the look in his eyes.

These were crazy times, she said to herself. She tried to blame her feelings on the excitement, the enormous turmoil that existed around her. But all that really existed was the touch of his lips against her cheek and the look of him asleep in the bed, relaxed and no longer the street-fighting revolutionary.

She spent the day in the darkroom developing the photos she had taken the previous three days. As she hurried home through the mangled streets, she glanced at a clock as she passed a store. It was past five o'clock. She had spent the entire day in the darkroom.

Her mind returned to Alain. Curious. She had forgotten about him as she worked. But now the thought of seeing him again made her walk faster along the glistening sidewalks. She found, miraculously, a *boulangerie* that was open and bought bread. The baker told her of a *charcuterie* that still had some meat left. She ran there and bought some stew beef. At home, she calculated, she had some spring onions, some spices. She would make a *bœuf bourguignon*. That should take away the chill, Alison thought.

At her building she sprang up the stairs, unlocked the apartment door, and ran in. She threw the photos on the bed and headed for the kitchen. Everything was there. Flour. Garlic. She peeled the potatoes, cut up the onions and sautéed them in butter, sliced and floured the meat, and then browned it. She added some red wine and set the mixture to simmer.

There was no electricity, but fortunately the gas was still on. She went to the telephone. The line was dead. Still on strike. It was growing dark. She found candles, lit them. She placed two of them on the table in the living room, one in the kitchen, and carried one into the bedroom. As she did this she found herself blushing. Her imagination had carried her far beyond dinner. She pictured herself in bed with Alain. He would be kissing and loving her. And there her mind had stopped.

She knew about sex, had heard the girls in the dorms talk about it. But Alison was still a virgin. "When the time comes . . ." her mother had once said vaguely, then stopped. It seemed as though the time was at hand, Alison thought, and *she* was totally unprepared.

Alain caught her in the bedroom. He burst through the door, waving the bottle of wine.

"*Voilà*," he said triumphantly. "Nothing is impossible." He glanced at her in the bedroom. "Ah," he said, grinning. "You have preceded me."

"There's no electricity. I was putting candles . . ." she said lamely.

"So I see." He sniffed the air. "But there is gas, and there is something marvelous cooking on the stove, and I am so hungry, I could eat—" He stopped. "I could eat *you*!" He lunged for her neck. The roughness of his beard scratched her skin, but she didn't mind.

"You seem so happy," she said, and then, making a joke, asked, "Did things go well at the office?"

He looked puzzled.

"Isn't that what wives always say to their husbands?" she asked.

"Oh, yes," Alain replied, and he joined the joke. He assumed the role of the tired businessman. "Well, it was—you know—meetings and conferences." Just as quickly he stopped playacting and grabbed her arm.

"I think we are winning since the leaders of the unions have joined us. The strike by all these workers must force de Gaulle to come to terms. Ah, I can't believe it. Us—we are such little kids—and the workers—they all look so old. Even our accents are different. Everything—totally different. And yet the anger is the same. And the determination. You should see it.".

"I'd love to," she said. Then, quite shyly, added, "I have something to show you. Can you see in this light?"

"Barely," he admitted.

She showed him her pictures. He looked at them slowly and in silence. Then he looked at them again, examined them more closely.

"But these are good!" he said in amazement. "They are better than that!"

"Are they? Are they?" Her voice changed, and she said in wonder, "They *are*. Yes, they are good."

"They are the truth. They show exactly what is happening."

She took the photos and put them on the dresser, then turned to him. He was staring at her.

"What are you looking at?"

"You amaze me," he whispered. "And you are beautiful."

She waited, then, for him to come to her, to put his arms around her, but he did not.

She served the dinner. He took his plate, but instead of sitting down at the table, he removed the candles and the two glasses and placed them on the rug. Then he sat down.

"It is easier on the floor. At table, it is too formal. I did not dress for dinner, as you can see. Have you a . . ." He was at a loss for the word. "*Tire-bouchon*," he said.

"Corkscrew," she translated. "Yes, of course." She brought it to him. He uncorked the wine and poured it. It was delicious and made Alison dizzy. She had not eaten anything all day. They both attacked the *bœuf bourguignon* greedily.

Outside the serenade of sirens and nightsticks and whistles and cries continued. But here, by the candlelight, they dined cozily.

Whether he was dressed for it or not, that was what they were doing—dining. Alison felt elegant. Her blond hair was spun gold in the candlelight, and to him she shone like a goddess in the night. They each put fork to mouth, raised a napkin. He watched the delicate movement of her arms. She noticed the hair on his chest. She drained her glass of wine. He poured another, and their hands touched. She sighed softly. Her eyes closed, and then his lips were on hers. She could taste the wine. She had been dying to feel his lips, and now she let her own lips explore his face. His hands were roaming her body. They kissed. She had been kissed before, but allowed it only through some kind of duty—college-etiquette, end-of-the-date kissing. Here she was kissing back. She was as greedy as he was. Before she knew it, she had stripped of her two sweaters and he was holding her breasts in his hands and kissing them. Putting his tongue to them.

Dizzy from wine and passion and exhaustion, she responded totally. They were naked and did not bother to move from the floor. He cradled her in his arms. It seemed to her their two bodies were glued together. And more than that she could feel his maleness, the hardness of him between her thighs. She thought she did not know what to do with her hands, but she was wrong. She stroked him, nuzzled him, felt the strength of his muscles, the smoothness of his back, and then her legs opened to receive him. There was a moment of pain, but it was a kind of glorious pain, and he was inside her, thrusting inside her, making love to her. She did not think of anything else from that moment. He made love to her, made her burn and pant and cover his face with kisses. Her body obeyed every movement of his, and then, as though a great barrier had been overcome, she cried out to him. Their cries mingled, their bodies mingled. This was ecstasy, Alison told herself. This was completion. This was the reason she had been born. To receive a man and give to him, to take him inside her and to gather his love.

And they were spent then, on the rug, both of them breathless from the passion that had engulfed them.

There was blood. He saw it.

"You— This was your first. I am so sorry. . . ."

"No! No!" She covered his mouth with kisses. "Nev

be sorry. Never be anything but what you are. You are my lover. My lover."

He carried her into the bedroom and they lay in the darkness. He cradled her and stroked her skin and whispered in her ear, and she found she was crying, and he was crying too.

"I love you," he said, surprised. "I honestly love you."

"Is this what it is? Is this what it always is?"

"No, my angel. It is almost never like this. This is something so special, so rare. You will never forget it, nor shall I. So long as we live."

Don't miss RECKLESS DREAMER, on sale July 15, 1985, wherever Bantam Books are sold.

LOVESWEPT

Love Stories you'll never forget by authors you'll always remember

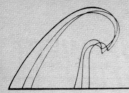

LOVESWEPT

Love Stories you'll never forget by authors you'll always remember

SPECIAL MONEY SAVING OFFER

Now you can have an up-to-date listing of Bantam's hundreds of titles plus take advantage of our unique and exciting bonus book offer. A special offer which gives you the opportunity to purchase a Bantam book for only 50¢. Here's how!

By ordering any five books at the regular price per order, you can also choose any other single book listed (up to a $4.95 value) for just 50¢. Some restrictions do apply, but for further details why not send for Bantam's listing of titles today!

Just send us your name and address plus 50¢ to defray the postage and handling costs.